CRUEL TALES FROM THE THIRTEENTH FLOOR

FRENCH
VOICES

FRENCH
VOICES

WINNER OF THE FRENCH VOICES AWARD
www.frenchbooknews.com

CRUEL TALES FROM THE THIRTEENTH FLOOR

Luc Lang

TRANSLATED BY DONALD NICHOLSON-SMITH

UNIVERSITY OF NEBRASKA PRESS | LINCOLN AND LONDON

Cruels, 13 © Éditions Stock, 2008
English translation © 2015 by
Donald Nicholson-Smith

An earlier translation of "Initiation,"
by Anne Kaiser, appeared in Fabrice
Rozié, Esther Allen, and Guy Walter,
eds., *As You Were Saying* (Champaign
IL: Dalkey Archive Press, 2007).

The translations of "Mad Love" and
"Rendezvous" in this volume were
first published in *The Brooklyn Rail*
(September 2009). "Mad Love" was
reprinted in *Brooklyn Rail Fiction
Anthology 2* (New York: BR Books, 2013).

The translations of "Face?" and "The
Lord's Day" in this volume were first
published in *Fiction* 54 (2008).

This work, published as part of a
program providing publication assistance,
received financial support from the
French Ministry of Foreign Affairs,
the Cultural Services of the French
Embassy in the United States, and FACE
(French American Cultural Exchange).

French Voices logo designed
by Serge Bloch.

Cet ouvrage a bénéficié du soutien
des Programmes d'aide à la
publication de l'Institut Français.

This work, published as part of a
program of aid for publication, received
support from the Institut Français.

Library of Congress
Cataloging-in-Publication Data
Lang, Luc, 1956– author.
[Short stories. English]
Cruel tales from the thirteenth
floor / Luc Lang; translated by
Donald Nicholson-Smith.
pages cm. —(French voices)
ISBN 978-0-8032-3747-6
(paperback: alk. paper)
I. Nicholson-Smith, Donald,
translator. II. Title.
PQ2672.A5155A2 2015
843'.914—dc23
2014049426

Set in Ehrhardt by Lindsey Auten.
Designed by N. Putens.

For Alice

Many fewer supports can be identified as the basis of the athleticism of the soul. The trick is to irritate these supports as one might lay bare the musculature. The rest is accomplished by cries.

ANTONIN ARTAUD, *The Theater and Its Double*

CONTENTS

TRANSLATOR'S ACKNOWLEDGMENTS

I am grateful to the French Centre National du Livre, whose grant (*bourse de séjour*) to me in 2012 much facilitated the present translation. I am also much obliged to the Cultural Services of the French Embassy in New York, and most especially to Fabrice Gabriel and Anne-Sophie Hermil, for very much more than the financial aid of this book's French Voices grant to the publisher. Lucinda Karter of the French Publishers' Agency, the U.S. agent for Luc Lang's work, has been a stalwart backer of the project and a good friend. For various forms of practical and moral support, I am much indebted to Donald Breckenridge, Cathy Pozzo di Borgo, Alyson Waters, and, as ever, Mia Nadezhda Rublowska.

Last but certainly not least, I must express my warmest thanks to the author, Luc Lang, for his help, patience, and friendship.

D.N.-S.

CRUEL TALES FROM THE THIRTEENTH FLOOR

1

UP↑ DOWN↓ FRAGILE

You must admit, these cardboard boxes are a nuisance—couldn't you get them out of the way?—wait! what about the cellar? no, it's already stuffed with boxes of bedding, things—stuff everywhere! she can barely get to the boiler—the attic then? no, the leaks, water gets in, it'll ruin everything, no, there's just no more room—there's still the dilapidated garage, but she wants to keep her car in there—I don't insist, zigzag my way through the piles of boxes to the toilet, impossible to get there discreetly—true, I hesitate to use the bathroom on short visits, it draws attention, but it's hot and muggy, I drank almost half a liter of water on the way over, can't hold it, excuse me just a moment—I'm back now, relieved—Antoinette rises with difficulty from her armchair, her snow-white hair impeccably done—she is wearing a pretty green-and-red checked suit, earrings, necklace, rings—she is offering to make me herbal tea? real tea? something warm anyway, and she is shivering, in full summer—oh, I never see her anymore! if it weren't for the dog—does that surprise you?—I know, Antoinette, I know—it's simple, nobody tells me anything!—I'm not unaware that "anything" refers to the life of her daughter and son-in-law but more painfully of her granddaughter. A kind of litany every ten minutes. Ask her to stay sitting down, I'll take care of making the tea—wait! look at this—can you see her there, in her schoolgirl's smock, with her smiling little face and her eyes?—she looks surprised behind her spectacles—how ugly children's glasses were in those days. Oh! my little granddaughter, such lovely hair she had already—her parents worked so hard, my daughter in a laboratory and my son-in-law with his studies—they didn't have the time, so I'd pick Alix up from school, fix her dinner, her bath, read her a book at bedtime, stories of Prince Charming that she always begged for—I know, Antoinette, she was always in your arms, your "warm arms" as Alix used to say—I almost raised her myself, that child, you realize that?—yes, I do—no, no, don't get up, I told you, I'll make the tea. Thread my way through the boxes again, to the kitchen this time, light the gas under a saucepan with a cracked, burnt, black bakelite handle, poke around among jars of crystallized preserves and cans of food for a few musty Lipton tea bags, freeze-dried contents as much food mites as tea—quick! pop them into boiling water, get an odorless, barely tinged liquid—tray, two-color plastic wobbly-top sugar bowl, teaspoons, oh yes! she wanted me to get crispy speculaas cookies, they are rubbery now—arrive with the tray, zigzagging, swiveling hips, oops! oops! catch my right foot on an enormous bag full of gym shoes and sneakers of every brand and color, fifteen or eighteen pairs of them, size 40, I know sizes—almost fall headlong over a chair, miss the back of it, but only just! steaming tea floods the tray, scalds my fingers, reduces the particles of the cookies to a brown paste—desperately I manage to deposit my delivery on the dining-room table, ouch! ouch! my thumbs are on fire!—you have to admit it, these boxes are a menace! Antoinette smiles—but what if this were you? your foot caught in that bag, your knee bumping into a cardboard box? boom! you fall, get burnt—disaster!

Boxes of clothes, shoes, fabric samples, rolls of material gleaned from markets at closing time, kimonos, saris, fur coats, airman's coats—it's like a warehouse here! is your granddaughter opening a store? no, the boxes in the cellar belong only to her daughter and son-in-law, they have no room at their place. On the other hand the ones up here are her granddaughter's, not the same thing. It's too small here for the endless stream of clothes. The house really has to be straightened out. Then, when it's done—but what will be done exactly?—she shrugs and waves her hand across her face as though batting away a fly. She has been wanting me to come by and pick up some boxes in fact, packed specially for me, double curtains and an eiderdown that I can do nothing with except take to a thrift store. She is obsessed with this, telephoned me every three days till I agreed to come, as though she wanted to entrust me with her will. For the last four months Antoinette has no longer been sleeping in her bedroom on the sole upper floor—the toilet is on the ground floor so her bed is now set up there too, in the dining room. More and more "troublesome" intestinal difficulties, so when I wake up in the night with my stomach painful and upset I haven't the time to get downstairs—it must be the tumor, Alix told her in a would-be reassuring tone, the one that makes your neck swell up like that—nothing out of the ordinary, in other words. But I never see her anymore, you know—nobody tells me anything, that's all there is to it!—they come through here like the wind, separately or together, daughter, son-in-law, and granddaughter, moving boxes, taking things, bringing more boxes, always in and out, secretively stocking up and removing stuff. And that's it! what do you expect though? at the moment my bank account is empty—zero! so Alix prefers to visit her aunt, who has ready money—she's the one now who pays for her trips to far-off places, her scooter, her rent arrears, because I can't do it anymore—don't tell me that surprises you?

We take little sips of our tinted water, munch on the non-inundated speculaas, the sun's violent but clouded rays filtering through the dirty windowpanes. The dining room feels dank, the burning liquid warms us up, sweat beads on our brows. Her only scrap of good fortune, as she thinks—the only one!—like a dove clasped between her two white hands, hands of the skillful seamstress that for long years designed, cut, and sewed Alix's dresses, skirts, pants, and coats—yes, her only good fortune is her granddaughter's regular Sunday visit to drop off the dog for her to mind because Alix works till Thursday and the house and garden seem to offer the simplest way to board the animal. This means that she sees her granddaughter twice a week—oh! not that Alix stays long, as you well know, always in a rush, friends all over the place, and as I say, no one tells me a thing—yes, Antoinette keeps on repeating—yes what?—her arrested state, her suspension between two stretches of time: Sunday to Thursday and Thursday to Sunday—she holds out her cup, I refill it with tea—the liquid seems to warm no more than her skin, her bones remaining cold, cold from a gradual chilling that is inexorable except for the spasmodic surge of warmth at the side of her throat, just below her right ear, whenever her lymph gland becomes unduly swollen. In a few months her home has been shrunk by her reduced bodily mobility. Upstairs the two bedrooms, hers and Alix's, where we slept for so long, are already given over to storage. It is not rats that proliferate but the trunks, crates, cardboard boxes, and bags of her encumbered progeny, turning her house into a vast left-luggage office, she herself epitomizing the putting of everything into storage until final clearance—including her own, in a box, completely cold. What gives her a kick, as a parting thumbing of the nose: when it is over, think of all those boxes they will have to move! in short a life of lugging boxes around for wandering good-for-nothings—feel pressure in my chest, hard to get my breath—she is shaking with cold—listen, Antoinette, it's so hot outside and you are shivering, why not let some sunshine in? but what am I thinking? why don't we put our hats on and go and sit on deckchairs in your lovely garden with its manicured lawn and flowering shrubs?—oh no, Lucas, it is too much of a wreck—what do you mean?—I get up, open the window wide, the dining room suddenly awash in the blazing summer's golden light. Lean on the rail, survey fifty square meters of lawn now horribly abandoned, which I had not noticed coming in through the courtyard—the turf marred by patches of yellowed grass with, in the middle of each, like poisonous hearts, more or less solid, more or less liquid or dried-up, dog droppings incorporating themselves into the ground. And beside the thirsty shrubs and rare flowers are deep holes and mounds of dug-up earth. So the garden is part of it too—repurposed as a latrine for a stashed dog. Antoinette is right, you can feel the end, an odor of damp cardboard, of warm paper pulp and glue, and a stink of dog shit given off by the earth in the heat of the sun. The saliva turns rank on my palate—I close the window full of a sadness that poisons the sensibilities, but not she, from the great depths of her nearly one hundred years of age: does it surprise you? picking up dog dirt to mow the lawn? filling in the holes almost every day? no, she doesn't go out into the garden anymore, that being by far the simplest—but surely, Antoinette, there must be some other solution? and—and Alix, couldn't she . . . ?—come, come, Lucas! you know her! you—you who love her so much!

2

Sniper

Been next-door neighbors for eighteen months, pre-war working-class lots, long narrow parcels, red-brick houses, semi-detached: iron railing on the street, little cement yard in front, couple of front steps, two rooms and kitchen on the ground floor, bedroom and bathroom upstairs, then in back the little garden 32.7 meters deep by 5.3 meters wide, just a strip of turf with in my case a lilac and a cherry tree—Jacky Houdard moved in with his five kids and wife, pregnant—perhaps time for them to check out contraception, but they went to church regularly—ha, ha, I ribbed him the other day, wink, wink, nudge, nudge, over a pastis and roasted salted peanuts, not the only thing you do regularly, huh? Jacky? huh? and I brayed hee-haw! hee-haw! just like a Tibetan wild ass—and his cheeks were burning, a little embarrassed smile, head hung, like someone caught with their hand in the cookie jar!

Washed-out red hair, pock-marked skin, features drawn by fatigue and strain, eyes abnormally large and bulging, like the eyes of a grouper through the porthole in an aquarium tank, he wore overalls around the house just as he did at his job at the Villepinte Citroën factory as a foreman on the C3 and C4 dashboard production line. A late addition to his life, his Mauritanian wife did housework wherever she could find it, six kids before long, rice and potatoes more often than lobster and crab—the house being too cramped, over seven weekends he had covered fifty square meters of his garden with corrugated asbestos-cement roofing atop windowless glass-wool sandwich panels and installed an oil stove: "the kids' room"—in a tone at once proud and guilty, have to provide shelter for them after all!—if I reported him for building-code violations he would have to dismantle his favela in short order, but I'm no monster—look at the energy and skill applied to making sure his offspring have a roof over their heads—the back door to the said sleeping quarters led out through a tool shed to the remainder of the lot, taken over by rows of potatoes—Bintge, the most productive variety per foot. Add seven chickens, a rooster, a front wing and fender of a Citroën BX, a set of tires, a drum of motor oil, some dismantled scaffolding . . . a gutsy guy, Jacky! hyperactive! works non-stop, treats his life like a cross to bear, which, at fifty, wears you down. Thanks to his anarchic/illegal structure I had him—any impoliteness, lapse, inappropriate action, daytime or nighttime noise, barking mutt, and wham! letter of complaint is off, in duplicate—I've got it all ready too, just needs dating—but, lucky for him, no hitch up to now—and he knows it, Jacky, his sword of Damocles—I brought it up with him, straight up, over pastis and pretzels one summer evening: very nice, but not so legal, is it, Jacky, huh? what if someone in the neighborhood was ill-disposed?! slam! bang! complaint lodged! your goose is cooked! but it's only visible from your place, Noël, so there's no risk—you're right there, Jacky! but suppose I had a cocktail party in the garden, a sort of neighborhood get-together, music to bring the summer in, with Monsieur Maurice, Rachid, Madame Gustave, Monsieur Zameczkowski, Hassan, and Monsieur and Madame Kourouma and their seven children—they would be bound to see the structure you put up, inevitable—but, hey, don't worry, Jacky, I'll keep a weather eye out—my tone generous, protective, as befitting my age—but he got the message, Jacky did—he sends his wife over now to clean my house from top to bottom, free, gratis, and for nothing, five hours a week, plus sewing, ironing, often even shopping—she is still built, young Alcina, thirty-two, never mind her regular deliveries, and if she wasn't seven months pregnant—even now, when I watch her in action, doing the housework, hips and backside swaying—but, hey, I can wait . . .

This afternoon, a Sunday too hot, too sunny, traveling funfair and dance on Place de la République, the smell of overripe underarms and moist crotches, steering my way through the crowds with a mental pince-nez, I stop at a shooting gallery, clay pipes parading lazily, bang! bang! bang! six shots equals six decapitated pipes, am an excellent shot even with these crooked popguns—the stall keeper not happy at all has to give me a jumbo-size plush toy, a pink Tele-tubby—suddenly I spot Jacky with his five brats between three and seven years old and his wife in the throes of naturalization. Beckon them over—chance to kill two birds with one stone: number one piss off the stall keeper, number two rattle the neighbors—switch to shooting at balloons in a black cage, bang! bang! bang! six times and six popped balloons in quick succession—the booth man can't believe his eyes, checks to see if the gun's barrel is perchance too straight. Right away, pick out a doll as ugly as the monkey-headed Teletubby, one forty-five centimeters long that whines mommy! pipi! hungry! milk! etc., gather up both toys and present them to the two oldest kids, girls of four and seven, with a sugary-emotional smile—they jump up and down for joy: thank you, Mr. Noël! thank you, Uncle Noël!—no kidding, Uncle Noël—and Alcina, her big eyes brimming with gratitude . . . ah! the bitch! those fleshy lips! it's not a balloon I'd like her to blow up! but now suddenly the other three kids, little boys, are getting jealous, pestering their father, they also want prizes—poor Jacky! his smile has disintegrated, he is stricken, he'll have to pay for everyone to shoot . . . and with his lychee-syrup eyes behind their bottle-glass and his serious strabismus he has no hope of hitting either pipes or balloons, and he knows it, knows that even with the luck of the cuckold he's going to throw money away, and he's broke but can't refuse his kids, who are in an uproar and at fisticuffs—darts me a panicked, imploring look, wishes, wants so very much that I shoot for him, ready if need be to pay me for the rounds—I make like I don't understand, abandon him to the gaze of his children, in his role as strapped, squinting, clumsy father—handyman is one thing, marksman quite another!—off you go, Jacky, have a good Sunday! leave him to it, blanched, stricken by the rapidly worsening family drama—much rather see him lose face with his offspring than report him to the building-code agency and make a martyr of him—ah, no! walk away, nice and friendly.

3

Left

It was mid-afternoon when the phone rang. For a long time. Was in the garden, spring sunshine, pruning the rose trees—by the time I got inside the house it was too late—I grabbed the cell phone from the sideboard, kept it on, slipped it into my pocket, and went back to my gardening—it had to be important, and it went off again immediately—I saw "Laure" appear on the display: yes?—hello Pierre, how nice to hear your voice, you've been forgetting me lately—yes, you're right—a long silence from her end—hello? hello?—in the background a dull sound, then her voice, sobbing: Pierre, oh my God! I can't take it anymore, I can't take it!—Laure, are you . . . ? what is it? hello?—she did not reply, went on crying—but where are you? I can't hear you! hello?—he doesn't want me to keep him!—what?—to keep the kid!—he, who?—Charles, he doesn't want me to! we . . . we're separating—she was crying, choking—but where are you?—I'm driving, on the freeway . . . can I come to your place? I don't know where to go, except to the devil—well, I'm not the devil, Laure . . . I'll expect you—she must have managed a smile, her sobbing had stopped—sure I'm not bothering you? never, Laure, you could never bother me—our friendship went back more than ten years now, a collusive friendship—we had worked together on a production at the Théâtre de Genevilliers, she on the lighting, I on the set design—the fact is, I had been in love with Laure since that time, though I'd never told her so—would have been useless, wasn't mutual, maybe she suspected something, but she soon fell head over heels for Charles, eight years ago now—I had no choice but to bow out, jumped at a chance to leave Paris and take a job in Strasbourg, to get away—you're where exactly, Laure? I told you, on the freeway! yes, but where? at . . . about two and a half hours from you, I think—speak to me, Pierre, say something!—you know very well it's dangerous to talk on the phone when you're driving, and—no, I have to hear you, I'm going crazy, talk to me, Pierre, talk!—no, Laure, it's too dangerous, you must hang up now!—listen, I think I have an idea—you remember that CD of Neil Young that I burned for you?—yes—you love that CD don't you? do you have it in the car?—I . . . I don't know—look and see, okay?—I could hear her rooting in the center console, things falling on the car floor, the noise of plastic on plastic—I couldn't stand the picture I had of her driving at 150 kph, flooded with tears, looking for a CD—I was terrified of hearing the sounds of an accident, a frightful screeching, in my ear—what the hell was I doing in the roses with my pruning shears, in my gumboots and old canvas jacket, what the hell was I doing?—oh, you found it? put it in the player, volume high the way you like it, and let yourself get into it—I'm waiting for you, take good care—when the CD ends, call me back okay?—yes, okay—she was crying, but she agreed—see you soon then—yes, very soon.

The garden was suddenly a desert without so much as a blade of grass growing, nothing more for me to do there, went back inside, doffed gloves, boots, jacket, and began waiting—two and a half hours, it would be late afternoon, she'd have the sunset, so beautiful, on the vines round about, must get her room ready, take a shower, shave, make myself presentable—hadn't seen her in six months, a telephone call now and again, her voice, sad at times recently it seemed to me, postcards when she was traveling—I was nervous about seeing her here, where she had stayed only once, with Charles, but overjoyed to think of her coming to take refuge at my house—I would be her recourse in her state of great distress—half an hour later, me in the shower, the telephone rang again—got out dripping, slipped on a robe, dashed over to grab the receiver, shit, it was Charles now—yes, hello, Pierre? not disturbing you?—no, no, I was in the shower—oh, so sorry, excuse me—I'm worried, you haven't heard from Laure by any chance?—no, why?—you don't know about it, but—we—we've decided to separate—gosh, how come?—too long a story to tell you now, over the phone—but she left here last night like a mad thing, I'm calling everywhere, can't reach her, I'm so worried—wanted to tell him not to worry, because she had decided to keep the child, but didn't dare, not my business—nor did I admit that Laure would be with me in just over an hour—up to her to call him or not—excuse me, I have to carry on going through the address book, talk to you later—fine, Charles, and do please keep me informed, or else I can call you—never really warmed to this guy, hard to say why, rather stuck up, a lawyer and investment counselor, sure of his competence, of his place in the world, of what he was meant to do, very reassuring for Laure no doubt—his admission that he was anxious was a first—but calling everyone in their address book, as he was clearly doing, was to say the least a convenient way of announcing the break-up: poor Charles, so worried about Laure's disappearance!

So I got dressed, shaved, readied her room (on the ground floor so that she could go out and come in freely), laid out towels in the adjoining bathroom, a bunch of jonquils in a vase on the chest of drawers, went back to the kitchen, put a piece of salmon on a plate to defrost, I'd bake it in salt, with sticky rice and sautéed wild mushrooms, uncorked a bottle of Saint-Estèphe and decanted it into a carafe, skimmed the newspaper, surfed the Net briefly, checked the forecast for the next few days, canceled several appointments and two dinners in the coming week on grounds of sickness—the fact was I was climbing the walls, stuck in time, time that wouldn't pass. She ought to have called again, should have arrived a good half hour ago—I had an urge to get on my motorbike and ride to meet her, then accompany her back, be her escort, a silly, childish idea—she had first mentioned her wish for a baby two years earlier, as I remembered, at a dinner party at their place in Vincennes with other friends, among them Charlotte, who was six or seven months pregnant—we all noticed distinctly how Charles had no reaction, a startling silence, as much as to say: she is saying nothing / I heard nothing / none of my concern—this despite Laure's looking at him and repeating how much it was now a pressing matter and a happy prospect for her, etc.—he did not even return her gaze, kept talking to Jérôme about enlarging the consultancy, taking on more partners . . .

As a lighting engineer Laure was capable of transforming a scene like a magician—using light alone she could make spaces immense, cavernous, or tiny, transform the actors' bodies into white, two-dimensional, and near-transparent shadows, paper cut-outs, or alternatively into thick, solid figures rooted to the ground, like golems—she could render any set almost superfluous—she would stride around the stage, go up into the flies, and climb among the structures suspended from a theater's ceiling with the agility of an acrobat or a mountain climber—indeed she went mountaineering several times a year. But why didn't she get here? the sun had dropped behind the vines, the last glimmers of its setting were fading from the horizon, she ought to be here—I didn't understand, but if I phoned with her at the wheel—oh well, too bad, couldn't wait, called anyway—at least it rang—rang but no pick-up! left a message: yes, Laure, this is Pierre, I'm worried because you are still not here, see you soon—hung up and resumed my anxious pacing around the house—a good five minutes went by—there! my cell's ring tone went off with its dated Brazilian music—but wait! Laure's name was not coming up on the display, instead someone with a restricted number was bothering me—I picked up, irritated: yes,

hello?—hello, is this 06.46.17.93.07?—yes, Pierre Andréas, that's
right—this is the Sarreguemines gendarmerie, you have just called
Laure Aldën, and yours was the last number dialed to her cell phone,
is that right?—yes, perhaps, yes, certainly, but your question makes
no sense—are you a family member?—yes, I lied. They had sad
news for me, Laure's death on the A32 highway—what's that? the
what?—yes, Mademoiselle Aldën was killed at 5:40 p.m. on the
A32, not far from Exit 16, as she was changing a wheel—I beg your
pardon?—her wheel, a flat tire on the offside front wheel, she was
struck and killed by a car traveling at more than 130 kph, must have
braked for at least a hundred meters, his original speed clearly very
high—Mademoiselle Aldën's car is intact, she had her cell phone
on the passenger seat, and—what are you telling me?—it had to be
a joke—what was he saying? that she was struck and killed? that the
car was jacked up, the nuts on the right front wheel loosened, that
she was continuing to unscrew them by hand? this was pure inven-
tion! laughable nonsense! suddenly, in the stiltedness of his serious,
even stony tone, I divined the uniform and the mustache—he told
me to calm myself, that he understood my distress, that was the
actual word he used, but this was none of his doing! calm yourself,
Monsieur Andréas, please!—excuse me, but are you telling me that
the car was undamaged? that she was run down changing the right
front wheel? that she was in the breakdown lane crouching down
between her Golf and the embankment, unscrewing the nuts?—we
are sure about the nuts, she was holding one tight in her clenched
fist—was he really saying she was struck by a sedan that didn't col-
lide with her car while she was between the right front wheel and
the embankment? so where was the sedan traveling? where? on the
embankment? that was crazy! and anyway I didn't give a shit about
his insane story, it was Laure who—are you quite sure that she
is . . . ? but then how come . . . ? I'm sorry, but your story is incom-
prehensible!—well yes it is, for everybody, because Mademoiselle
Aldën was changing her wheel in the fast lane, the left lane, coming
off a long bend, yes, the fast lane, pulled over as though she were on

an ordinary road—she had turned her engine off, had time enough to position the jack, loosen the nuts, get out the spare wheel, and jack the Golf up onto two wheels, then she was struck, it was dusk—the windows were rolled down, there was music playing, deafeningly loud, inside the car—it was dusk, he said again, in the left lane . . .

4

Initiation

Always choose the emu enclosure (emus belong to the ratite family) down below the path—the area is bounded not by railings but by a turf-covered ditch, so the heads of the brown animals with their bluish necks can sniff around the top of the grassy bank at the foot level of the passing visitors—the little kids are delighted to halt here with their parents or grandparents—when one of them stands within the emus' reach, fascinated by their almost ostrich-like heads, black plumage, staring orange eyes, I go over to the ditch, stop a few meters from the child, step down onto the embankment, grab a handful of grass, and offer it, ostentatiously, to the nearest emu, who relishes it, asks for more . . .

No, don't have much to do with the mammals, mostly take care of the feathered creatures: ashen cranes, marabous, pink flamingoes, birds of prey, parakeets, macaws, cockatoos, can't list them all, the zoo houses a vast range of species—clean out their cages, feed them grain, fruit, raw vegetables, meat, lumps of suet, and all kinds of things, check the health of every specimen—yes, I've been working here for twenty-three years, exchanging the customary chirping salutations almost every day, especially with the parakeets and parrots: hello to you, oh Jacquot! hello to you, Émile, you old aristocrat!—I love this formality with the birds—twenty seconds later, to get the conversation going, I say: you have sweet dreams, don't you?—which is not true! birds have nothing but shreds of ill-defined dreams, and as for me, now I'm old, I don't dream anymore, eyes open in the blackness of my white nights—but who cares!—"you have sweet dreams, you know?"—I used to break my back trying to teach them this—in fact it was supposed to be not "t'as de beaux *rêves*, tu sais?" but "t'as de beaux *restes*, tu sais?" ("you still have your good looks, you know?"), with reference to the ripe old age attained by parrots—they will still be there the day I retire—"you have sweet dreams, you know?"—oh!!! the fury the first few times: why do you say *rêves*? it's *restes*! the zoo's veterinarian, an expert on the phonetics of talking birds, claimed that they have serious difficulty pronouncing diphthongs, triphthongs, and sibilant-plosive clusters, as in re*st*, *str*ap, mu*sk*etry, or *c*orsair, but that the labials *p, b, v,* as in rê*v*e, *b*oat, Val*p*araiso, or *p*irate, are like child's play for them, even though they lack both lips and vocal cords—it's on account of their respiratory system!—the famous avian syrinx at the junction of the two bronchi enables them to modulate many sounds and syllables . . . or so said our vet/poet—in the end though, *rêve* is more joyful for me than *reste*, more exhilarating, more evocative of the future, brings me back to a time when I longed to depart for marine and tropical horizons traversed by multicolored birds—as it is, here I am still in temperate climes, surrounded by Parisian vegetation and concrete rocks—at least I have the company of birds from five continents with which to live out my days . . .

Getting back to the emus (one of the closest descendents of the dinosaurs!), offering the tuft of grass to one of them about six paces away from the wonderstruck boy—nothing is more tempting to a little kid than holding out food to an animal—he has an irresistible compulsion to feed, to tame, to become the special interlocutor, the intimate friend of a nature hitherto mute and indomitable, to discover his own humanity thereby—in short, to repeat the action of primitive man domesticating nature and possessing it with his imagination, millennia of work buried in our reptilian brain and rehearsed tirelessly by the child—so now the boy in his turn grabs a tuft of grass, as his parents often do for him, and holds it clumsily between his tender little fingers—it is at this precise moment that I straighten up, ready to walk away nonchalantly, the tyke holding his tiny hand out toward the head of the emu, which reacts swiftly, its neck undulating like the body of a dancing serpent, opens its powerful beak, and chomp! closes it violently upon the unforewarned fingers of the frail pale hand, slicing open the flesh of one, two, three fingers until they bleed—inevitable, given the internal structure of the bird's beak—terror, tears, pain, streams of blood, smiles all gone, kid traumatized, parents blanched, distraught, happy moment demolished—already turning my back, heading off to get on with my work, a little, irrepressible smile of satisfaction on my lips—you don't hold your hand out any old how! as if the whole world were at your beck and call! no! reality! a lesson in reality! no more dreaming! I chuckle silently—this morning, in bright sunshine, my 368th victim!—and here comes the mother chasing after me: hey! what about your uniform? yes, you, Forest Green!—do you belong to this zoo, yes or no?—yes I do, body and soul! to the birds, yes!—that's how you set an example? on purpose? to get my son bitten! you lousy bastard! I saw you! I'm going to report you!—slam the metal service door of the Lemur Rock in her face—off limits to the public, you crazy bitch!

5

Private Life

The supplier was on the phone with me, we were having a big fight—two minutes *if* you don't mind! I went into the boss's office, I had no choice, he was away—looked for the mail confirming the order (for 120,000 euros' worth of material!) due for delivery today, not the Ides of March! found it, but also came across a super-confidential file that was super-interesting to me—God willing, it might just save my bacon—I had to get out of a tunnel, be done with the streak of rotten luck that had plunged me into this dark, stinking pit for almost an entire year—the Christmas before, brutal layoff with the financial liquidation of IG Tube, my employers—Alain throwing me over for a little slut, twenty-two years old, barely pubescent, deleting us, our two kids and me, from his existence, and going off to the Côtes d'Armor, where his company had set up shop, to live out his idyll—had not seen him for six months, the only news coming via his lawyer in the shape of preparatory divorce papers—could no longer keep up with the rent on our apartment, the only lifeline being this provisional contract, four months to prove myself—now done—ten-hour work days, not to mention the files I took home to work on at night after the kids were in bed—poor little things, eight and ten—my task at the company was to set up telephone and computer networks in the new headquarters of Electronics 3000 so that the relocation of the firm's 276 employees could be effected without their activity level suffering more than the five days of authorized slowdown—well, mission accomplished, mein Führer!—on my own except for Cindy, a young secretary, and a couple of temporary interns as well as my boss, Alex Grosser, who supervised the job. I was exhausted. Two kilometers of swimming every Friday afternoon and a fifteen-kilometer jog on Sunday mornings had kept me in shape—at thirty-six I am still well proportioned—and there was the rub—Mr. Grosser had his eye on my ass—at fifty-five he was discovering a new youthfulness—slim, blue-eyed, always tanned, he drove a sports car, and he would have loved to fuck me on the spot in his office, no fuss, ceremony, or oratorical preliminaries—never mind his pretty little blonde in her early thirties.

Last week there was a cocktail party on the managers' floor to celebrate the opening of the new headquarters—all the executives, department heads, and upper management types were there for *petits fours*, duck liver mousse, taramasalata turning fuchsia-pink, runny cheeses, and the kind of mediocre champagne that makes your breath resemble the last burps of an empty soda siphon—looking me in the eye, he whispered: good work, Laetitia, a flawless performance—we make the final decision about your definitive employment contract next week, and I'm confident that—his hand was on my hip as he said this, close to squeezing the top of my ass cheek—I was backed up against the appetizer table—there were plenty of people there, but no one noticed his errant hand or his shameless scrutiny of my cleavage—he made a return foray later, drunker, his hand this time in the small of my back, urging me to let him drive me home in his new Porsche—message received loud and clear: my cunt for his prick, and a permanent employment contract in my pocket in ten days' time—didn't say no, just that I couldn't accept the ride, my two boys were waiting at their grandmother's for me to pick them up and get them to bed quickly, school tomorrow—another time then, Laetitia!—with pleasure, Alex!—next week?—why not?—I had to play for time, for Christ's sake, play for time—what could I do? I couldn't get sick or say the kids had the flu, not just a few days before the signing of my contract—I felt my back was against the wall, wanted to sabotage the brakes of his Porsche, put arsenic in his Alka-Seltzer, infect his cashmere scarf with the smallpox virus, or castrate him at the crucial moment—dream on, poor Laetitia, dream on!—next week, he had insisted—okay then, I'd hang in there. And then on Monday I came across a confidential file in which a few letters and invoices showed clearly that an advance agreement had been made between Grosser and Galactic.com, a large telephone and computer hardware concern that had supplied and installed cables and terminals for our new building, to settle at a far higher price than those offered by Galactic's competitors—something like, oh, say 300,000 euros—so I dug around a bit in Galactic.com's org chart, and there was his wife! Teresa Grosser-Helbach, majority shareholder, a fact that might just interest our board of directors—and I now had the wherewithal to temper Mr. Grosser's ardor—I photocopied the file, stashed the documents in a safe place, and eventually accepted his third dinner invitation, for Thursday, after citing (1) the dentist on Monday (ah! if only I had a mouthful of rotten stumps and breath rank with decay) and (2) my boys Tuesday and Wednesday evenings—which left Thursday, when it was more or less implicit that he would exercise his *jus primae noctis*—then I brought up my discovery of apparent corruption around the invitation to tender, trying to get to the bottom of the Galactic.com business: but surely, Mr. Grosser!—I mean Alex, sorry!—their proficiency is highly dubious, I'm sure we must have had to work twice as hard with them as with the competition, check every detail—well, yes, that was why you were here, Laetitia, to take care of everything!—and they are supposed to be the most expensive in the market! I really don't get it!—you are certainly well informed!—and it's just that there are rumors,

Alex, and—Grosser did not blink, seemed sure of himself, hinted that a structural alignment of Electronics 3000 and Galactic.com might be in the offing, two companies so perfectly complementary, could soon be a European leader!—your position will be bursting with prospects, Laetitia!—shit! shit! this was fucked up!—went off and delved into the org chart of our own shareholders, and bingo! there was Alex Grosser, one of the three largest, as if he were getting ready to buy our company using his wife's—this was trouble—the smaller shareholders would be obliged to follow, and my big gun was changing before my eyes into a water pistol—no more leverage now over this bastard on Thursday night—could I tell him over dessert that I had a urinary infection?—he wouldn't give a damn—an STD?—wouldn't believe me—God was definitely not on my side! I would—would what?—Monday I stewed over it, didn't sleep a wink until daybreak—and then eureka!—went Tuesday evening to see Éléonore, my friend who is a riding instructor for the Union of Outdoor Sports Centers, a great horsewoman and practitioner of dressage, sometimes with the Gruss Circus, and resolved to go for broke—I really wanted that position bursting with prospects—but not his prick between my legs!

Here we were at the Grand Veneur, the Master of the Hunt (even the name of the place made me want to throw up), a chichi restaurant not far from the Place des Ternes with large white napkins, four crystal glasses, eight pieces of silver cutlery, waiters in penguin uniforms—I was already choking with anxiety—and Alex Grosser playing the regular, as though this were Monsieur's canteen, at two hundred euros a pop, and the maître d' and master sommelier dancing attendance, falling over themselves with obsequiousness, sizing me up with their gutless eyes, seeing if Moo-sieur's latest whore was presentable—we were seated off to the side, in a dark corner, away from the noise, at a candlelit table—wow! how original! Grosser ordered lobster to start, followed by wild boar, *grands crus* as accompaniment, champagne as apéritif, *natürlich!*—how, at his age, could he still go for this kind of masquerade? he was more creative when it came to money matters, but his piles of dough could not enrich his imagination—poor guy! talking to me about his liking for authentic, healthy, and light food (couldn't help wondering how the game was going to be prepared for his vegetarian palate) and about his passion for travel to faraway places—but then who, dear Alex, would not relish good food and trips to the tropics if all they had to do was sign checks?—he paused for a hundredth of a second before bursting out laughing: ah! Laetitia, you are some sort of woman!—then he was off again, describing his last vacation in Mauritius, from which, yes, I remember him returning burnt to a crisp in the middle of January—do you like water-skiing? he was very good at mono-ski—really?—in Madagascar he would rent an outboard, and Jérôme, yes, the financial director of Electronics 3000, would steer—I see—and what about Formula 1 racing, do you like that? he never missed a Grand Prix, always watched from the VIP enclosure, traveling even as far as Argentina!—and, oh yes, he wanted to tell me about his little private jet—well, little, yes, but it seated four, it was a cheetah, a fine machine! and so much simpler for traveling—he would visit the Atlas Mountains, fly over the desert, at least once a year—*indispensable* for his mental equilibrium, given all the stress, all the responsibilities—I wondered: was he giving me his sports-and-leisure CV or an archeological history of modes of transport?—he probably expected me to identify with his luxurious, glittering lifestyle, devoid of children, devoid of love, just one son left behind twenty-odd years ago with the mother somewhere in back of Nice, a son to whom he tossed a few euros for his tuition—because he was no deadbeat, Alex, he did the right thing! irreproachable when it came to springing for the mother and child—time is money, is that it?—why yes, Laetitia, every hour that goes by!—yes, but do you think you can buy time, I mean, yours and other people's?—of course! because they work for me, and why do you suppose I have a plane? it's so I can fly over the desert in barely four hours—oh, I see, I hadn't thought of that—phew! we were almost at dessert, I couldn't swallow another thing, no thanks, just a sorbet, yes, from

Berthillon, but of course, Jesus wept!—he had been circling around the subject of the Electronics 3000/Galactic.com deal for at least five minutes—you mean a merger?—no, no, a close collaboration, synergy in a sense—yeah, complete with layoffs!—absolutely not! all our personnel are top-drawer—out of the question to sacrifice all that brain power!—the career you are being offered, Laetitia, is like a Ferrari—you are coming in at just the right moment—however, two of our directors are away at the end of this week, so, as to your contract, we won't be signing it till next Tuesday, at the latest—oh! you slimy snake, you bastard, I thought, you want to screw me again this weekend, you want my ass 24/7 through Tuesday, with your trumped-up postponements!—don't make such a face, Laetitia! tomorrow or Tuesday, what's the difference? you are a pretty young woman with your whole life ahead of you, what's five days more or less?—no thank you, no liqueur—he settled the bill, I noted the total: 679 euros, cheap at the price—let me take you home, sweetheart—in your Porsche, Alex, otherwise I'm taking a taxi!—he burst out laughing—wondered was his vanity piqued or had he grasped the irony of my response—he was so infatuated with himself—helped me into my coat as I was putting it on, his hands lingering on my shoulders, waved regally to the staff—the maître d', hips still swaying, cheeks still drooping, led us to the revolving door of the flower-bedecked lobby, the parking valet opened the doors of the red Porsche already idling at the curbside, and we were off! Monte Carlo Rally toward Courbevoie, where I still live in a nice flat, mortgage payments in arrears and bailiffs and banks on our back, because, yes, we chose Courbevoie to be near my mother, who loves to take care of her grandchildren—and since Alain left she's the one who sits them whenever I'm—like that evening—and takes them to school next morning—it's a modern building, well designed, with balconies overlooking a private back garden—Alex parked meticulously, turned the ignition off—I thanked him profusely for the lovely evening, had my hand on the door handle—I hope, he said quickly, you're going to invite me up for a nightcap?—piss and shit! here we go!

even till the last second I had hoped he might let me escape—God had forsaken me!—aside from tea, I don't have much to offer you, Alex—actually, I'm the one offering the nightcap, if you want—and from the back of the car he produced a bottle of Dom Pérignon already frappé and snug in a chiller sleeve that he must have bought at the restaurant—you think of everything, don't you, Alex?—Laetitia! it's not every day that we celebrate a great event!—what event?—well, our collaboration present and future! and this first evening spent in your delightful company—okay, that's it, then! let's go! I extricated myself from the car—hang in there, girl! no way round this!—ninth and last floor, panoramic view of the Place de la Défense, extra-large living room, three bedrooms—we shed our overcoats, I bring champagne glasses from the kitchen, we settle down on the leather couch, Alex congratulating me on the spacious interior, so very tasteful (*sic*)—which doesn't surprise me of you, are you the owner, when did you buy it? what about the neighborhood, etc., etc.? three or four minutes of this, we drank a toast, he took my hand, he was in a hurry, I let him take it, he refilled our glasses, the champagne was delicious, made it easier to smile, sparkle, be bright and charming, we clinked again, he kissed me, too fast, too keen to French me, darting his tongue into my mouth, his mouth too moist, disgusting—my glass is empty, Alex! more champagne, more!—looking at me pruriently, his eyes full of lust and his lips reddened, he poured with one hand and with the other kneaded my thighs and burrowed up my dress—neutralized him as best I could by taking off his jacket, tie, shirt—his left hand kept returning to the hollow of my thighs, groping for my pussy, his right hand squeezed my breast like a lemon, his geography of the caress sorely lacking, he licked my neck—I had him bare-chested now, he was indeed slim and muscled, his musky smell off-putting to me—we were obviously made to fuck each other . . . not!—oh! Laetitia! Laetitia!—yes, that's my name—Laetitia!—yes, okay, Alex, yes—I was in a red bra, a thigh-length black dress—my thighs were firm enough to prevent his hand getting into my panties, where he would have found lips dry, not to say freeze-dried, a clitoris withdrawn deep into its shell, a vulva tight as a strongbox—his mouth was suckling at my upper breast, my hands were at work: belt undone, fly unbuttoned—your shoes, Alex, your pants, hop to it! off! out of them! feverishly he pulled at his Westons, not bothering to unlace them, wrenching them off—I had his weapon in my hand ... ah yes! no doubt about it! Alex was getting a hard-on, yes, a hard-on! now was the time: lick his squeaky-clean ear and whisper: just a moment, darling, I'll be right back!—what? well, hurry, you naughty girl!—don't worry, hand-some!—rushed to my bedroom, the props ready, must be quick! black thigh-boots, black g-string and bodice, all in soft leather, chrome chain belt, four times around the waist, so heavy! gloves and wristlets with hooked steel points, lace-up mask, collar with ethnotrash lion's teeth, riding crop in the left hand, short whip in the right—thank you, Éléonore, for the three hours of training each day, including Tuesday—now I knew how to snap the whip, cut a cigarette paper clean in two, slice a piece of cloth, or (almost) write a Z with the whip like Zorro! should I take a look in the mirror? shit! some woman! so it's all or nothing, huh, my little Laetitia?—I dashed out of the bedroom, he had his back to me, his dick in his hand, I crept up behind him on tiptoe, cracked the lash, he jumped, turned, I snapped the whip once more, missing his nose by three centimeters, and again, grazing his hand and opening a deep gash in the leather of the sofa—Grosser's face had melted down, he was staggered by the spectacle before him, couldn't believe his own eyes, but turned to face me, slowly, as I went on whipping the air, just catching his shoulder—I stood erect, legs apart, unsmiling—on your knees! lick me, Alex, lick me! he was out of it, trembling, this wasn't his thing, he had lost his erection pronto—I brought the riding crop down on his back, ouch!—come on! come on! obey!—he got down on all fours and licked without conviction at the top of my thighs—the whip cracked again, skimming his white backside, another whack from the crop fell on his flank—get up, for Christ's sake!

fuck me! come on! do it! hard, Alex, like a dagger, like a sword, get right inside me, to the hilt, Alex, run me through! go to it, big boy! I spread my thighs wider, pulled him up by the hair—he stumbled, cock limp, shriveled, knees together, shook his head no, stupefied—is it you, Laetitia?—this is how I like to fuck, Alex! full force, come on, for God's sake, like a bull, Alex! go on, force your way in! what are you waiting for?—another time, Laetitia, I've had too much to drink tonight, I feel ill—he was getting into his raw-silk boxer shorts, his pants, his shirt, his shoes, and stuffing his tie and cufflinks, along with his socks, into his pockets—some other evening, then?—yes, yes, okay, I'm sorry—when, Alex, when? I'm all wet, Alex, I want you, shit, when?—don't . . . don't know, Laetitia, don't have my appointment book . . . I—his camel-hair overcoat was draped over his shoulders, he was stumbling backward toward the door—the lash scythed the air for the last time, shattering a vase to signal my displeasure—with my other hand, dropping the riding crop, I made a big show of scouring my cunt, arching my pelvis, growling with the fury and frustration of a tigress in heat—good night, Laetitia, good night, and he closed the door behind him, phew! he was gone! all-or-nothing had worked! the jerk must just love inflatable dolls that panted under his chief-executive's thrusting, but here, with me, all that had gone down the toilet in seconds—I had made a wager, he might have been aroused—but no, Sacher-Masoch, Venus in furs, just wasn't his cup of tea—he was bound to leave me in peace until the contract, wouldn't come back to the subject of his sudden deflation, it would be our little secret, one hand washing the other—I won! I won!—then came a little voice from behind me: is that you, Mama?—turned round, my two boys stood at the hallway door with their grandmother! hey! what in God's name are you doing here?—please, Laetitia, don't swear! and take off that mask, you're scaring us!—oh yes, forgive me! but what in God's name, what in God's name are you doing here?—calm down I tell you! there was a fire in the building, two floors down at Monsieur Per- cheron's—we had to evacuate, so we came up here to you, what else!

I'm sorry, I can't tell you just how sorry I am!—we were sleeping . . .
it was, well, it must have been you cracking the whip that woke the
kids, me with my sleeping pills and wax earplugs—they got me out
of bed, but it was too late, they were terrified, horror-struck—I
didn't have the time to shield them from this performance—now
Thomas, from the superiority of his ten years, was looking at me
strangely—come on, back to bed children! broke in their grandmother, tomorrow is another day—she slammed the hallway door
and took them to their room, leaving me on the edge of the sofa,
fucked—it was all fucked up—took off my gloves, gulped the last
of the champagne from the bottle, lit up a joint, started crying,
crying a river . . .

6

Flux

Too much, it's just too much! Ticketed three times in four months
for not respecting pedestrian crossing?! for refusing to yield to what?
to pedestrians? who are not on wheels, who are not vehicles, who
are just foot-borne elements, entirely extraneous to the traffic! yet
they still have priority, apparently, in every automobilistic context!
and convictions don't come cheap: 250 euros plus three points on
your license, and 3 x 3 = 9! I responded accordingly and began by
way of a gigantic excess of zeal to demonstrate how irreconcilable
these two mobile universes are—for the last five weeks I've been
systematically letting any waiting pedestrians cross the street in front
of me—the drivers behind me could honk and shower me with the
wildest abuse; I didn't give a shit, I was letting those people cross!—I
even anticipated people's desire to enter upon hydrocarbon-rich
roadways!—please, go ahead, after you, and so forth!—which earned
me emphatic thank yous, salutes, moms telling their brats what a
model citizen I was, if only all drivers were like me, say thank you

to the nice man, blah, blah, blah! — and old people calling me a fine fellow, a real gentleman, a decent soul . . .

Last month, on a long, straight, clear street without intersections or traffic lights, a one-way street on which drivers tended to speed up considerably, with just one pedestrian crossing halfway along, I spotted two young guys with their stupid iPods hovering, in polar fleece jackets four sizes too large and their jeans hanging halfway down their asses, waiting, presumably, to cross — I was going fast, so I pulled up in short order, brake pedal to the floor, coming to a halt precisely at the edge of the crossing — an idiot scooter guy had been tailgating me for the last three hundred meters, continually trying, like a hysterical wasp, to overtake me, but the space was too narrow — no room, you asshole! no room! is what I was thinking as I watched him in the rearview mirror — as I say, I pulled up sharp at the crossing, and the fellow behind, after ramming straight into my rear bumper, took off skyward, rolled over my hood, and ended up like a dizzy, disjointed puppet on the aforesaid pedestrian crossing — the two kids stopped their jittering instantly, took their headphones off, and rushed toward the body on the ground — I burst out of my car shouting, enraged: what's the idea, you want me to run over pedestrians?! you stupid idiot! — said idiot got painfully into a sitting position, took off his helmet, and freed a head of long, dark hair . . . a pretty little mixed-race Latina à la Jennifer Lopez, a little pale from fright, shock, and pain — the idiot was a female idiot no older than twenty — I took a walk around my station wagon — no, the bumper was not bent, though the scooter was in smithereens, my hood on the other hand was badly dented, the roof antenna ripped off, I realized, by the airborne body — what about the safe distance between vehicles? the speed limit in built-up areas? not so much a spot of trouble for her, more like deep doo-doo! — the kids had carried her onto the sidewalk and sat her down with her back to the graffiti-packed wall that concealed the Regional Express Rail line — the older one, in his black beggar's hood, had unclipped his cell phone and was about to call emergency services — her leg is broken, man!—whoa! just a minute, before you call, let us take care of the mutually agreed statement of the facts!—okay, but why did you pull up, man?—to let you guys cross, obviously!—we weren't going to cross!—what do you mean, not going to cross? standing right at the crossing? you must be fucking joking!—hey! keep your shirt on, buddy! we're calling medical emergency; my old man's a nurse, that's an open fracture!—oh yes, the bone sticking through her pants! okay, time to get rid of these pests—I flashed my press card, really quick, put it away, and growled "police!"—with their joints dangling from their lips and their pockets full of grass, the pair lost no time waving to Jennifer Lopez and scampering off without trying to push the river—I went and got an accident report form from the glove compartment, began filling it out, returned to Baby Doll, who was just getting ready to pass out—oh no you don't!—extracted her pocketbook from her jacket pocket . . . great little tits, nice and firm, my God! okay, I know, not the moment!—hey, little girl, just sign here at the bottom, press hard, you're making two copies, then I'll call the emergency people! right, good, you can go into your coma now; I'll fill out the boxes for you—the paramedics will be here in three minutes—she was having trouble breathing, turning white, greenish—don't move, I have water in the car, and chocolate, I do have a heart, etc.

That was a test run, by no means a master stroke when you think of the time wasted: accident report, emergency services, repairs to the BMW—no, not perfect, but this afternoon was more exemplary—a rare opportunity, the timing delicate: a four-lane avenue, repeat four-lane, which is important, red light just changing to green, an old couple getting ready to cross, a car visible in my rearview mirror far off but coming up fast, planning to pass me in the left lane, me not moving on green, instead rolling down my window, calling to the seniors: go on! go on!—usually people say thank you but decline to cross, too dangerous, no, no, the little walking-man sign is red, no, thank you, sir, it's too late, we're in no hurry, thank you!—but this little couple, standing there huddled under their umbrella, the rain falling hard, she with snow-white, blue-rinsed set hair, he with a checked tweed cap and a cane, both in soft penny loafers taking on water, both shivering, frail, timid, did not dare refuse, I being so assertive: absolute priority to pedestrians! you are the living memory of a vanishing era! hail to our seniors! glory to the old! when an old person dies, a whole library is burnt to the ground! etc., etc. And by way of a benign joke: make way for youth! they were flattered, smiling and nodding—I was the center of their attention as they passed in front of the hood of my wagon, then there they were in open country, setting off with little steps across the left lane under their umbrella, their eyes fixed on the asphalt so as to sidestep the puddles—the damn fool behind, intending to sail past me on green without slowing down, suddenly saw the old pair right in his path, braked reflexively on the wet roadway, which did not do it—he was about to make mincemeat of them beneath his wheels—he wrenched his car violently to the left and found himself in the middle of the oncoming traffic, felled a motorcyclist, pulverized a Smart Car that he bore forward with him onto the sidewalk, gathering up two pedestrians and a baby in a stroller before ending in the frontage of a baker's shop: shouts, screams, the racket of twisted metal, shattering shop windows, smoke, blue sparks shooting up from the pastries—the old couple were unharmed, except for palpitations and Parkinsonism, petrified, trembling like autumn leaves with their umbrella, which the wind had turned inside out: hey! old fogies on parade! what's this crossing the road with your eyes closed, like daredevils?! you're completely irresponsible! playing with the lives of other people . . . I'd lock you up if it were up to me! in an old folks' home! this neighborhood won't have bread for several weeks because of you!—and I started off, nice and slow, perfect! innocent as the driven snow! Vivaldi, *Four Seasons*, maximum volume inside my car.

7

Mad Love

I still have the view of the sea—I run the film over and over, in a loop; I'll die with the thing running through my head—when he appeared that late afternoon in July '63 he was Apollo himself, a radiant golden sun—supporting his old parents on either arm, they looked for a table inside, near the window, then went outside again and picked one on the terrace, on the sidewalk, to be near the bustle of the Boulevard Saint-Germain—I still have the view of the sea—I don't regret a thing; the mobile home is comfortable, I have the car for doing the shopping, and my lab keeps me company, faithful as a dog should be—there is no explaining it: when the English say "to fall in love" they mean falling *into* love, but when you really fall in love you do so literally—it is like falling in battle, falling at the Front, struck down in war—Angelo ordered a rum with Easter Island fruits, his father a Rackham the Red rum, and his mother a cinnamon-vanilla Caribbean rum—I'll never forget him ordering, bursting out laughing over the names of the drinks, but yes, of course it's me, and my husband, who make them up!

brown curly hair, big Mediterranean-blue eyes, shy, with a smile at once embarrassed and winning—eight years younger than me, a kid—we laughed together over the rum menu, but all we needed to do was look at each other to laugh—we both knew that this was for life, at least almost—they were all tanned, the father dry and gnarled as a walking stick, the mother almost hunchbacked, half toothless, her head covered by the black shawl of the eternal widow—peasants up in Paris visiting the capital and trying a little rum—Angelo came back the next day, on his own, and every day after that, always sitting at the same table—I was the one who served the customers on the terrace—Georges said: your beauty is permeating Saint-Germain—they see you and descend like locusts on a wheat field, and more power to us!—poor Georges—not easy to engineer a first date when you are chained to your work, and before long the lies bloomed, venomous toxic flowers—we had opened La Rhumerie in 1949, on April Fool's Day, ah spring! I was nineteen, Georges twenty-eight, we were married that same year—we had them all for customers: La Greco with Gainsbourg and Raymond Queneau, Boris Vian, Montand and Signoret, Sartre and Beauvoir, Jeanne Moreau, Miles Davis double-parking an endlessly long pink Cadillac on the Boulevard, Maurice Ronet, Michel Legrand, Françoise Dorléac, Picasso—the list went on and on—Signoret, though engaged to be married at the time, used to swap glances with Montand from afar, then they would sneak off together—we were onto them so quickly that before long Georges and I became the mail drop for their billets-doux and assignations—yes, it was a fine decade, feverish, bursting with energy and new beginnings—why did Angelo have to turn up?—true, I've kept the view of the sea!—a Corsican shepherd, my poor Juliette? what the hell are you going to do with a shepherd? a Corsican? in the Corsican mountains? don't tell me you're going to rewrite *Astrée* for us?—no, Georges, I am going to relive it!—we were divorced, I sold my share in the business, no bagatelle at the time, and went off to set up house with Angelo in his shepherd's homestead: a mud floor, whitewashed walls, one table and four chairs, a bed, a fireplace, a terrace shaded by vines and fig trees, altitude six hundred meters, and a view of the sea—I put my money into a building above Calvi, a dozen rental apartments—a decent income over and above the goats and sheep and our pastoral idyll day after day—it lasted for eighteen blazing months and it felt like eighteen days—we buried his parents the next year, his uncles came down from Paris—Angelo grew tense, anxious, irritable—the long absences called for by the management and migrations of his flocks became more frequent—he refused to let me go with him—for a whole year I was consumed by waiting for him week after excruciating week—don't worry, my Juliette, everything is alright—the worst words imaginable, the kind that mire you in fear and suspicion—and then, one summer evening on the terrace in the sweet air redolent with the scent of figs, amid the chattering of the cicadas, an anxiety-stricken Angelo made me a murmured confession all about illegal arms, tobacco, and alcohol trafficking, the shifting alliances he suspected, and clan and family betrayals—but we have enough money, Angelo! why take such risks? stop it! take care of the sheep! we don't need anything, we are fine just as we are—he got angry, a man of the South, the proud torero—it's not *my* money! and he spat—a month later a black pick-up turned onto the track to the house and drew up in front of the terrace—it was a stultifying sunny afternoon, the countryside shimmering in a furnace of immobility—here and there small fires were laying waste to the scrub—three hooded men climbed from the truck dragging Angelo, his face slashed, left eye bloody, cheekbone exposed and lips mashed, and pushed him into a chair—are you Juliette Desforest? they tossed a bundle of notarized documents onto the table and held a pen out to me: sign, hurry!—sign what?—the sale of your building, and hurry up about it!—no, I said, no!—one of them withdrew an enormous chrome-plated pistol from under his jacket and without hesitation put a bullet into Angelo's knee—I had blood on my dress, my shepherd was rolling about in pain at my feet, not a cry from him, not a moan—don't sign, Juliette, he muttered—but I signed briskly, trembling, every last document, sheet by sheet—they gathered the papers up, slapped me about, pushed me into the back of the place, raped me each one of them, laughing crudely, obscenely—hear that, Angelo, how we make her come, your bitch? she is panting like a rutting she-goat!—I passed out, remained unconscious for a long time, woke up late in the day to a silence like that of a devastated village, of people massacred—everything was overturned and smashed, and outside—outside, the dog, goats, and sheep lying in pools of blood, and—and in the fig tree, the head of my Angelo, just the head, hanging by the hair, the face unrecognizable, horribly swollen, eyes gone, a vision of absolute barbarity, and as for the body it was never found—I took his head down from the tree, the head I loved so, oh my God! wrapped it in a white cloth, held it on my knees and in my arms till night—and when they buried him I insisted that his coffin be full-length for a man his size, even if nobody on the island was unaware of the details of the crime—the murderers, I shouldn't wonder, were in the funeral procession . . . I left Angelo and that malignant island behind and with the little money still in the bank I bought this scrap of land above Antibes, and that is my story!

You are making things up, Juliette! you are making things up!—it was not like that—true, you left Georges and La Rhumerie, you abandoned everything, family, friends, to go off with your shepherd to the Isle of Beauty and live there in that house perched above the sea with the sheep and goats and the smell of figs and eucalyptus—true, the pastoral idyll lasted a few months—but when you were married, you and Angelo, your investment in that little apartment building above Calvi became part of your joint estate—you were co-owners, and Angelo lost no time mortgaging the property, which was eventually foreclosed on by the banks so thoroughly did he dilapidate your income to settle his gambling debts—he told you that he had doubled your livestock, that he was negotiating to buy a walled-about farm where he would build a sheep pen and a cheese-making facility, that the operation would shortly expand into breeding and before long become a paragon among Corsican food-farming concerns—what tormented you at the time were the painful days of waiting, the evenings and nights spent alone while he took care of the construction, traveled far afield to buy new stock, or supposedly led the flocks from one mountainside to another but never took you along—and then when you got pregnant your loneliness was still more acute, your abandonment more desperate, though you still had no inkling of the imminence of ruin—true, all you had left was this hovel, a table and chairs, a bed, a fireplace, and, outside, that heavily perfumed terrace whence to admire the view of an endless sea—true, one afternoon a black car raced up the track, and true, three hooded men dragged Angelo out of it, his face swollen from their beating—true, they knee-capped him with a high-caliber round, and true, they raped you before him in that dog-day heat—and true, you lost your baby and you lost consciousness, but true too, your Angelo was betraying you with any girl he met during his bar-hopping nights—until, that is, the time he slept with the wife of an underworld boss and his death was decreed, and death in the worst way: beating, castration, decapitation—they must have played football with his head before hanging it from a branch of that fig tree—your beautiful Angelo, the love of your life for whom you gave up everything—true, you still have the view of the sea, a photograph taken from up there, with the fig tree of the hanging head in the left foreground—you can see the stone terrace, a wild-rose bush, the garrigue falling away, and the paradisiacal blue of the sea filling the whole width of the picture under a radiant sky that bathes the image in a crystalline light—yes, you still have the view of the sea, an enlarged photograph pinned up opposite your bed in this miserable room with its piss-yellow walls and its sole window, narrow and barred, giving onto the courtyard of the hospital, itself crammed between a dump and an expressway interchange in an industrial suburb of Toulon—when are you going to face up to the reality of your life, Juliette?

Face up to what? Except for the horror? What do you suggest?

8

The Cold Chain

I had a deep love for my wife!—still love her—didn't deserve this!
fifteen years of marriage without a hitch—and without children—we
tried for them, at least for one! we plotted temperatures, calculated
the respective trajectories of sun and moon and their passage through
points x and x', copulated at the median time of equinoctial ebb
tides, stored sperm samples in the freezer and injected them into
her womb at a precise hour/minute/second—it was like launching
a space station into orbit! result? zilch, blame falling variously on
ovulation problems, on genetic incompatibility, on deficiencies of
the spermatozoa, even on their motor inability to swim against the
current, which prompted my boundless admiration for the exploits
of the Alaskan salmon—in short we were told all sorts of things in
every version and variation—ah, if only a divine child had been
produced by our union, then perhaps we—anyway, we have had
many dogs; four still enliven the garden and the house: a labrador,
a fox terrier, a Pyrenean shepherd, and a chihuahua—Brigitte is a
mother first and foremost—she has to bestow her love upon live

beings, some more alive than others, skate and eel being a long way from us as compared with dogs! and when I say "mother," don't get me wrong, because Brigitte is also a woman!—very much a woman!—always in black stockings and suspenders, half-cup bra, deep cleavage, miniskirt, stiletto heels, and most of the time her crotch open to the four winds—hates to feel confined, so she says, and underpants, even the lightest, even the most diaphanous, give her a kind of mental allergy, an urticaria of the brain so to speak—and that way too, she adds with a smile, the door is open to any impromptu erection—as when, suddenly, I come up behind her, toss her pleated skirt over her head, uncover her white buttocks framed by a black garter belt, and bend her over the Empire sideboard as she offers me her vulva—or when I get on all fours under the Louis XVI table while she is eating dinner, or at the foot of the French Restoration–style plum velvet sofa as she pages through her magazines, her chihuahua on her shoulder, and off she goes to seventh heaven—she's hot, my Brigitte—I have already caught her by surprise polishing her shrimp on the upholstery of the Napoleon armchair—she ordered me to finish the job—instantly! if I wanted to be part of the incoming tide—I was anxious, stressed out by work, took part with tongue and fingers only, lingual and manual coitus, mere lip-service, pun intended—listened distractedly to her yelling, her gut-felt yes! yes! oh yes!

We met each other in the most improbable way—as the representative of three Northern European aquaculture companies, salmon, trout, shrimp, I deal with purchasing centers all over France—my job is to pitch the quality, freshness, and low price of the product, the customer appeal of seafood—crossing my fingers, have never had any serious setback in thirty years as a salesman and am still up for it! meaning eighty-five thousand kilometers a year on the road—that night, a Friday the thirteenth (spring of '86), I had a breakdown with my Citroën, a metallic-navy-blue CX, brand new! a suspension leak! impossible to repair it that evening, was well and truly stuck in Besançon, took a hotel room, at random, on a historic square where the cheese market and a country dance were being held, with the odors of reblochon, morbier, and cancoillotte practically wafting over me! I was bored, idled, sitting at the window with my elbows on the cast-iron guard rail, piling up butts, and contemplating the multicolored Chinese lanterns, the dancing couples, the children scampering about near the dance floor, and the local band shimmering with sequins in the spotlights. I love to dance: waltz, rumba, tango, rock, ska, twist, jerk, in fact any way of jiggling elegantly to a musical accompaniment—so to combat my distress I put a tropical suit on over a sand-colored polo-necked sweater and went downstairs and hung about by the dance floor—noticed a young red-haired woman, about twenty-six, with voluptuous, sensuous moves, a liana, a naiad, apricot skin beaded with an evening dew, a flowered, light mid-thigh-length dress, full round breasts, braless, fluttering just beneath the print material—I with my own flutters, a tightening of the throat—four or five horny, ungainly males hopping around her out of synch with the music, stiff as the handles of kids' shrimp nets, pants too short to go fishing, shirt collars broad as tuna steaks—living proof that ridiculous is not a fatal condition! pushing my way through the pack, I invited her to dance—she smiled, yes, danced like a bewitching siren, a wisp of alga in the tide, undulating, fluid—I was forty-two but had a Turkish sailor's hard-on, an irreversible cramp, a schooner's foremast in my pants—ah! Brigitte!—we met again at the next night's dance, pursued our initiation ceremony in my room all day Sunday, canceled my meetings for the next week—she lived small in a tiny furnished apartment overlooking the river, worked as secretary, supposedly, for an old admirer, a healer, medium, water diviner, a sort of town luminary with the mayor's and the prefect's doors always open to him—she had already bidden farewell, on the eve of her eighteenth birthday, to her adoptive parents, a couple of farmer-woodcutters settled not far from the Swiss border—I gathered that the old satyr of a father and his older son had severely abused her from her tenderest age—I piled her into the CX with her little sea-green suitcase and took her back to my house in Villeneuve-Saint-Georges—we were married the next month, onward and upward!—mind you, if I am describing the idyll of our incredible meeting, so out of the ordinary (brought about, think of it! by a leaky suspension), it is because . . . well, because . . . perhaps it was just a matter of hormones, but after I came upon her, on my return from a business trip, rubbing her clam on the edge of that armchair, I developed a kind of anxiety—putting aside the plum velvet upholstery marked with a kind of colorless patina of clam juice, my God! because of all her—but no! it wasn't that, just a sort of dull anxiety—so I tried to straighten things out, have her attend to her hormonal imbalance! and then I stopped being away for so long at a time, paid her all kinds of attention—one Sunday recently she was laying out in the sun, asleep in a deckchair, wearing a red silk babydoll, the Pyrenean sheepdog between her legs, his muzzle virtually in the crotch of my shepherdess, both of them sleeping the sleep of the just, innocents—such a charming scene, combining as it did flaming red hair, pink flesh, red silk, and a long-haired ivory coat in an almost savage harmony—I grabbed my camera—but no, my artistic intuition cried out that something was missing! the white terrace, the wall of the house, it was all too mineral, that was the problem! in the rediscovered harmony between woman and animal it was nature that was missing! nature! so, silently, soft-footed as a cat, I placed all the potted flowers I could find around the deckchair—the sleeping bodies soon lay in the balm of multicolored surroundings—click! click! I began taking photos from every angle, climbing on a stool for plunging, even overhanging shots, click! click!—oh my God! she was opening her eyes, awakened by the sound of the camera, moaning about being dragged out of an erotic dream, and true, her lips were moist and swollen like ripe fruit—she noticed the rows of flowers all around her, pushed the shepherd's head away, leapt to her feet, a hand still between her thighs, working her clit—Maurice! shit! Maurice, what the hell is this pantomime?! you're embalming me like a mummy, covering me with flowers like a showbiz star with a pulmonary thrombosis; it's a funeral wake! you're off your head, I swear to God! do you want to cause my premature demise? don't look at me with those dried-fish eyes!—what?—yes, just what I said! from selling fish and talking fish you've turned into a fish—you have the brain of a cod—get away from me! she kicked at the plant pots, trampled the flowers—it was horticultural genocide, Vietnam bombarded by defoliants—bitter saliva filled my mouth, and I slapped her face twice, hard enough to loosen her molars, ripped off her babydoll, flung my Brigitte down amid the chaos of plastic planters, scattered soil, and tattered leaves, and ravished her in a humus of crushed petals—we were drowning in the cloying sweet odors of geraniums, gladiolae, hydrangeas—she scratched at my eyes, my cheeks, my lips, screaming bastard! yes! yes! harder!—the cod humping the trash fish—is that it, Brigitte, is that it? but oh! the tremendous motion of those flanks, those hips, that pelvis!—our four dogs in a circle around us, their butts on the fake marble terrace floor, looking stricken and yelping from time to time—we got out of it okay that day, with our spectacular coitus amid the plant pots, earth, and flowers, more like an episode of "the life of wolves" than of "the life of fishes," in any case so abstract!—but the horticultural moment nevertheless disrupted our relations: we became more mistrustful, more suspicious of each other, and, how shall I put it? it coincided dead on with Brigitte's tumble into her forties, which put her through a metamorphosis, threw her into a kind of cannibalistic rage, a feverish, suffocating urge to devour the whole world—her canines grew longer till her mouth looked like a moray eel's—as I suggested earlier, she seemed unhappy and lost, so I shortened my trips even more, which led me to surprise her with the electric-appliance repairman, the plumber, the mailman, the doctor, the priest, as though she were sabotaging the stove, the fridge, the TV, breaking faucets, bunging up the pipes, forever signing for registered mail, and suffering from problems not only of the belly and the ovaries but also of the soul! all at least once a week—she could not abide being alone for a single day, despite the company of our four dogs—had she not begged me to buy a fifth, a doberman? and male to boot!—indeed, she would receive her repairmen in spike heels, stockings, garter belts, and rustling satin négligés—I'd find her on all fours with her head under the kitchen sink learning how the plumber uses the snake and unclogs the P-trap, or on her knees, hands pressed together as in prayer, confessing at the feet of the priest, who would be sitting nonchalantly on a stool, or again, stretched out on the Louis XVI table while the doctor listened to her heart—that's no way to dress, Brigitte! in the end I smacked her a couple of times, told her to cover up!—and the priest said nothing? just paid close attention to you? yes, she sobbed, he closed his eyes to follow me better, he called for God's grace—her face burning, cheek swollen, lips gaping, she whispered to me with a half-smile: don't worry my shark, my leopard, it's you that I really love—she got the message and took to wearing a dress! and then, very gradually, the electric appliances did not break so often, as if the impedance of the electromagnetic field of my nymph's body had changed; the drains were less frequently blocked, as if she were no longer, in some hypnotic state, tossing panfuls of rice into the kitchen sink and leaving cotton balls in the washbasin; eventually her soul itself seemed to get lighter, purer, her ovaries to ovulate better—no more technicians, plumbers, priests, and doctors coming to the house—the very factor, though, that ought to have set off alarm bells for me . . .

This is how it went down: in mid-June I returned from a grueling trip to the Limousin, where I obtained firm orders for 900 kilograms of salmon, 450 kilos of crayfish, and 1.5 tonnes of blue trout—pedal to the metal, devouring the autoroute, my siren's breasts and hips a holographic vision on my shatter-proof windshield! wanted to get home that same day, a Thursday, as quickly as possible and spend three impromptu days with her! ah! her ass! the nape of her neck! her pussy! a real revival of my flame!—and there she was, the devil! flinging her arms about my neck, her thighs about my waist, a medusa, naked in a sort of mauve gauze—I was not expecting this, stumbled backward—only thanks to my long experience as a rugby player was I able to bend my torso, push forward with my toes, and regain my balance—then we both toppled onto the French Restoration sofa over the backrest: oh! the little scorpion fish, her feverish gestures becoming more rapid amid her swirling veils!—ripping off my fly buttons and pulling out my prick and sucking at it, lips like a goby's on the glass of a fish tank—what an extraordinary reunion! when you thought about it, after fifteen years of married life, this was really fine, or so I told myself as I inundated her radiant face with spunk—moving on, that Friday morning with Brigitte sleeping in the innocent disarray of an angel come down to earth I crept away on tiptoe to go and top up on groceries at the Vélizy 2 shopping center—I was euphoric, grabbing up *grands crus*, sole, lobster, crab, oysters, the wherewithal to feast for three whole days—back home by noon, put the key in the door, heard a hoarse, harrowing scream, opened the door to find the mailman staggering about in the hall, his face a death mask, no kidding, pale as a ghost, his young curly headed Sicilian's countenance chalky white—he came forward doubled over, as though his innards were about to fall out, not a word, just a terrifying croak—I stood back, transfixed, to let him past me—he went out, thought I saw blood dripping onto the lawn—he dragged himself to the yellow mail-delivery van, took off at top speed, steering wildly and weaving like a drunk—letters scattered all over the place—panic-stricken, I shouted: Brigitte! Brigitte!—silence of the grave—Brigitte!?—yes, *liebling*, I'm in the bathroom, be there in a second!—oh, alright, but Christ!—went into the kitchen to put the food away—she found me there, all smiles, naked except for a coral slip with orange tints, high heels, and gray stockings with seams—what's up with the mailman? he left the house in a hell of a state!—oh really? I didn't notice—yes, like he had the runs! dysentery! he was bent in two—spasmodic colitis, perhaps, mephitic, for sure!—maybe even Mephistophelian!—at which we collapsed into laughter—she went to work on my crotch, sitting on the edge of the Formica table, her cunt gaping, hot, enough said—later we made lunch, a banquet—I drank a lot and plunged into a siesta several hours long, exhausted by my week of work and my wife's ardor—awoke at nightfall, Brigitte snoozing on the living-room carpet in osmotic embrace with our four dogs—wandered into the kitchen, popped a beer, started clearing up the mess, too much food still cluttering the table, decided to freeze some of it, opened the freezer, stuff had been sitting there for so long—sorted things to make room, throwing away leftovers we would never eat, came, right at the back, upon five polystyrene containers with curious labels: Gérard/13 March 2006, Yvon/12 April 2006, Simon/13 April 2006, Victor/13 May 2006, Matéo/13 June 2006 (which was today!)—and under the plastic wrap, carefully arranged, like pike quenelles whitened by the freezing, were five dicks, pricks, phalli, tools, peckers, schlongs, lingams, johnsons! the whole thesaurus ran through my head and down my spine in an icy stream—but yes, five ready-prepared dicks in their original wrappers, guaranteed fresh, source and tracking details noted on the package—five dicks severed by bare teeth, those of my moray I had to assume, and now my hands were trembling, almost dropped Victor's contribution—stuck the whole lot back into the depths of the freezer, closed the door, was overcome by convulsive Parkinsonian tremors, drowning in a wave of defeat and bitterness, swamped by a piercing and painful thought: this was grounds for divorce, wouldn't you say?

9

Sunday

The three-room apartment under the roof was in a filthy state—rust stains covered the washbasin, the bathtub and the toilet alike had a mat film turning light brown, the said washbasin was blocked up, the kitchen sink was leaking, the lino was curling up, yellowing, the paint on the sloping ceilings was blistered, that on the walls flaking—listen! I'm not going to start repairs when I'm about to move out, am I?—what about the table? and the chairs?—I gave them to Yolande, don't need them anymore—because, considering that she was moving to his place—well, think about it: he has everything in his house, makes no sense me landing there with a massive oak dining-room table and my six chairs—yes, but where did she eat, considering that there was no table in the kitchen either, where could she write a letter?—she had her stool, and her knees, quite adequate for the meantime—you say "him," you say "he"! but who is him/ he?—he is Jacques!—I see, and he lives where, this Jacques?—he has a beautiful house in its own grounds at Saint-Cloud, he is a doctor, director of a clinic!—and when are you moving?—Sunday!

he has friends with a moving company, they'll come on Sunday, which is their day off; there's less traffic on the roads—Sunday is tomorrow—yes, and I'm all packed, can't you see?—indeed, I could see her whole life contained in twenty or so cardboard boxes and two suitcases—corner cabinet and shelves had been emptied, not a single photograph, not a single picture on the walls, not even a crucifix, nothing at all—only her bed sheets remained, along with a plate, a salad bowl, a knife and fork, and a few thrift-shop clothes, the same old clothes, in the empty wardrobe in the bedroom.

I saw her again on Sunday night, sitting on her stool near the front door, her suitcases at her feet, in her dirty-beige raincoat, all ready to leave—they didn't come?—they are on the way, I tell you, stuck in a traffic jam, people coming back from the weekend—has Jacques telephoned you?—there's no need, I know they won't be long now—this was not happenstance: on an earlier Sunday their van had broken down—the Sunday before they had a flat—and the Sunday before that they lost their way in the suburbs, went round in circles for a few hours before giving up in discouragement and going back home—give me Jacques's telephone number; I'll call him and see what's happening—but she didn't have his number, it was always he who called—we mustn't bother him, he works so hard you know.

It was now three years since they met, crossing paths on Rue des Chrysanthèmes as they went in opposite directions on either sidewalk, she on her way home, he going to the station, catching each other's eye across the drenched roadway on a cold rainy afternoon, and she knew that he was the one, right away—and then what?—well, that's all, but that was not bad, wouldn't you say?—and he knows your name, and your telephone number, and address?—oh, he is not like your father; there are no flies on him, definitely not!—my father, who took care of her shopping, her taxes, her mail, who comes running over at the slightest health concern?—oh, she accepted all that to make him happy, but for her it was an almost intolerable burden—but Jacques, Jacques was different, Jacques had the solution! and anyway she and he did not need the telephone to communicate—yet she had said that Jacques had gone round in circles without ever finding her street, Rue André-Jumeaux, number 13, pretty easy to remember!—yes, it was strange; I never understood what happened—a month ago, she had climbed down the metal fire escape, slippery and ill lit, yes, around midnight, with a flashlight, and stationed herself for a good half-hour at the entrance to the street to signal him and show him the way, like a lighthouse in the storm—the poor man! he was wandering around helplessly—I felt anger sweeping over me because she had been navigating between cardboard boxes for three years now, the fridge had been unplugged for two, for a year she had been without table or chairs, and six months had gone by since the hot plate was tossed out, her clothes folded up in her suitcases, and since she had taken to dressing like a derelict in some kind of sweatsuit or pajamas, baggy and shaggy—you just don't understand, my own little boy!—right! I'm only fifty years old!—you don't understand! he was seriously ill, with cancer, how could he come to fetch me? tell me that! the state he was in! I had to be patient, I took care of him, from a distance, now he is cured, we'll be able to start a new life, a happy life! you'll see, my darling, a real family life—but for God's sake, it's nine o'clock at night! you don't move house at night, and on a Sunday!—listen, just leave me alone, he is coming!—her features were tight, her face contorted, and her eyes, brimming with fury and near-hatred, shot daggers at me, skewered me, scorched me, killed me—do you hear me? leave, if you're here just to interfere with me! let me live my life!—all right then, see you Sunday?—no, I'll be gone! but don't worry, I'll come and see you, with him, you'll see, he is a wonderful man!

10

Air Conditioned

The figures were not good—the production manager was screwing up—overcome by euphoria at the previous year's numbers, he had convinced us (not me!) to invest heavily in a diversification of our heat-and-eat cassoulet and lentils line: with knuckles/with sausage/ with pork shoulder; and country kitchen/artisanal/quick-serve/ vegetarian—he even added an exotic *chili con carne* version with red beans!—the analysis of the target segments seemed consistent enough, but the extension of the offering muddled the brand image and its impact, which had always been based on just two formats, glass jar or tin can, whether for sauerkraut, cassoulet, flageolet beans, green peas, split peas, or lentils—two formats, period! the outlay on promotion was also very onerous, and after eight months of mainstream distribution we had made no progress in market share, even lost ground to traditional products! we were in the shit! I never liked the guy, with his Boss and Armani suits, figuring himself for a revolutionary when it came to cassoulet!—okay, so he scored a king's ransom of a mortgage on his apartment in Neuilly, and his wife was supposed to have given birth to triplets—shouldn't have stuffed her with hormones! I couldn't give a fuck, we mollycoddled him, he's fired, he can go and get himself a job managing some grocery store around here—anyway, if his future employer is fool enough to contact us to check out the professional history of Monsieur Jérôme Guichard, I'll torpedo the dude in the worst way—he's lost us too much money, the competition is beginning to get wind of it . . .

It is a senior position and it pays very well, and the lucky person who lands it heads up all the product managers, negotiates with the suppliers, and travels around the production facilities in search of greater productivity and more appetizing tastes. It was my job for a long time until I became managing director, with two associate directors, and above us a board of shareholders and a chairman—there are times when I want to roll up my sleeves and go back to working at that—I find them so damn incompetent—all of them! too apathetic or too much for change at all costs—We put it out to tender and had five solid candidates, three men and two women, and we left with them on the 6 July for a three-day seminar at a luxury hotel in Yvelines—at the end of it we'd know who would replace the aforesaid Guichard—I went with my human-resources director, my sales director, and three assessors from ID Engineering's recruitment advisory committee—eleven rooms had been reserved, along with two meeting rooms, the whole ground floor turned into an assessment center! The five candidates were all around thirty, all well turned out, no ostentation, wearing suits, pantsuits, dresses, blazers—I ruled two of them out right away—Joseph Traoré, a Malian by extraction: couldn't see any relationship between a black and cassoulet! what if he was an animist and started invoking the spirits of earth and water to improve harvests, or offering us comparisons between the spirit of the cow and the spirit of the pig, and given his shoe-polish skin I could hardly see him inspecting production sites, dealing with agricultural cooperatives—give me a break!—as for Sephora Aménidès, never mind her flower-pattern dress, her chignon, her jewelry, and her apple-green blazer, she was as fat as a pig and pimply to boot, obviously ate badly, maybe too much of our own products or too much junk food, in any case the wrong sort of food in the eyes of the food-processing industry—the two of them would have done better to stay at home—just my opinion, of course, and I said nothing, minded my manners—we were at a table by the swimming pool with Perrier and fruit juice, in the morning sunshine—I introduced my three assessors, Brigitte, Marc, and Alain, and my directors, Philippe and Jacques, and gave a brief outline of the purposes of the seminar, went over each day's schedule, and handed out a summary of the tests, the point being to break the ice by means of a frank discussion—and to cheer our little group up I lost no time announcing that there would be a break between 2 and 4:30 p.m. in which to enjoy the hotel's facilities (swimming pool, sauna, jacuzzi, massage parlor, eighteen-hole golf course), to relax and de-stress—all meals were generously covered by our company; only the rooms, at 130 euros a night, were charged to the candidates—I spotted my Malian swallowing hard, a few drops of sweat on his brow, blecch!—that's how it is, I signaled him silently, electromagnetically, when you try to play with the big boys—he caught my meaning and looked down at his shoes, elegant ones by the way, John Lobb knock-offs most likely—the candidates were smart enough to realize that assessment had begun the instant they set foot in the hotel lobby, and that this informal meeting with its holiday atmosphere was itself an evaluation. Okay, let's go guys, settle into your rooms, we begin in Room 106 in half an hour. The other three candidates seemed like better prospects: Julien Lafarge, twenty-nine years old, the youngest, with fair, wavy hair, firm jaw, gray suit, smiling, prepossessing—Ismaël Abderhamane, thirty-six, first-generation Arab, seemed serious, athletic, elegantly dressed, easy talker, able to get dialogue going immediately—Elsa Kaufmann, thirty-one, blonde, also tastefully turned out, charismatic, very beautiful, a sort of Madonna in the grand manner, a devastating sex appeal that telegraphed "do not touch."

The first day was devoted to individual and personality tests—the in-basket test made it possible to identify the first shortcomings—the scenario presented is a return from vacation to confront a desk with mountains of hard-copy mail and a full email inbox—the question is how to deal with all this under pressure during the first hour back at work, how to analyze, assess, and take decisions, which tasks to execute, which to delegate, what appointments to make, and in what order. The candidates had at their disposal a computer and an electronic organizer, and the purpose of the test was to gauge their ability to handle relative urgency—in no circumstances should personnel issues be delegated—such matters had to be treated personally by the department head! young Julien panicked, and Sephora wanted to delegate everything, cool, sugar-coated, uninvolved—the others made out—as for the break at poolside, it was very instructive: Joseph kept his suit and tie and shoes on, sweating beneath a sunshade and plowing through Ulrich Boehhm on the market-research company—Julien, more laid back, sat in shorts on a deckchair paging through the financial papers with his iPod plugged into his ears, and Sephora scored points by scoffing chocolates—only Elsa and Abderhamane actually got into the water! good swimmers, and Elsa's body was a dream—a good thing I had my dark glasses, because I couldn't take my eyes off the naiad.

Next, in late afternoon, we gave an intelligence test to assess (1) emotional stability; (2) social intelligence; and (3) professional conscientiousness. Joseph, Elsa, and Abderhamane did badly on SI, but it was easy to confirm the fat Sephora's sense of duty, so strikingly absent in the morning, during the in-basket exercise, when she delegated in all directions—as for ES, Joseph Traoré and Ismaël Abderhamane, so far as I could judge, did not have much of a sense of self-worth, which was strange. Our first dinner, as is usual on these assessment-center occasions, was rather stiff—in fact everyone seemed to have a broomstick up their ass, and there was a dawning of tension between the candidates, an excellent sign! in two days they would be at each other's throats for the position, which paid 69,000 euros per annum not counting the productivity bonuses paid out in good years and bad, adding another 40 percent to the salary.

The next day the sun was still with us, took my breakfast with three candidates: Elsa Kaufmann, her voice warm and caressing, an exciting conversation about bioenergy, beginning of a boner; Sephora, armpits sour, Chanel No. 5 notwithstanding, told us her dull dream involving yellow and green caterpillars overrunning her body and leaving her covered with boils (no comment!); and Julien, who talked of nothing but stock prices and the inevitable rise of Carrefour hypermarkets, about which I couldn't care less—it's far too early for us to be looking for a stock market valuation—this was a day given over to group exercises—in the morning our five hopefuls had, first, to discuss a subject of a general kind, rather dopey (are highway speed limits justified?), and, second, come up with a subject themselves that was, let's say, more technical and professional—their subject: how to develop a strategy for wide distribution of a new food product targeting children. The atmosphere grew competitive, thus fully justifying our use of group work—we were able to tell right away whether the participants respected the basic principles of constructive discussion while at the same time vying for leadership.

To our great surprise the first contribution, breaking the ice, came from Sephora, the second, more predictably, from Elsa. Joseph often had good strong arguments but stated them so baldly that others were crushed—young Julien could not make himself heard and failed to intervene at any point—Abderhamane had the knack of involving all the speakers in the conversation, and Elsa was amazingly good as chairperson, organizing the discussion and summing up conclusions and results—We were beginning to form an opinion of the candidates, and, feeling too tired, I withdrew during the two o'clock break and went for a nap, leaving the assessors and the human-resources and sales directors as laboratory observers of a new soap opera, "Of Mice and Men." Coming out of my room about four, I gathered from Philippe and Jacques that there had been bitter argument between Sephora and Elsa over a moisturizing cream that the one had used without the other's permission, and that Joseph had been roundly scoffed at by Julien on account of his strong liking for French songs—I rubbed my hands together, this was all going great, and yelled, "Let's go!"

To explore the theme "Are you a committed team player or just a sheep?" we handed out index cards, box cutters, glue, and scissors and asked the candidates to construct a bridge eighty centimeters long and sufficiently strong at its midpoint to bear the weight of two glasses of water: who would design it? who organize the work? who plan? who carry out the plan?—young Julien Lafarge was an excellent designer, the sort who loves scale models, while Joseph executed the tasks required, the cutting out, the assembly, with great care and with Abderhamane's solid help—the two girls, willing as they were, were out of the picture, reduced to moving the air around like workshop ceiling fans, Sephora after the fashion of an agitated hysteric, Elsa more suggestive of disgruntled idleness—we applauded everyone at the completion of the project, then moved on to a role-playing session concerning a new product to be made at one of the company's five sites—which factory head would succeed in getting his or her site chosen?—an awfully informative confrontation as to who was going to take the prize, because you had to get an idea as soon as possible of the interests of the other participants, you had to know how to forge alliances, you had eventually to reach compromises, get contractual agreements down on paper, and use visual aids, such as flipcharts—Elsa and Abderhamane immediately sought to ally with one another and let one hand wash the other, Joseph tried to get Sephora on board with him, but she couldn't see herself alone on a boat in the middle of the ocean with a negro, and Julien, wanting to be the wily Master Fox, ended up as the gullible Master Crow—decidedly, the favorites for the position were becoming clearer by the hour—dinner was more relaxed than the day before; we were getting to know each other—the candidates were scattered among the directors and assessors; I had

Elsa to my left, Abderhamane to my right, pleasant conversation with both, talk of new technologies, genetically modified organisms, European Union legislation—I had asked the kitchen to arrange for dinner on this second night to be centered on pork, which let me observe Abderhamane avoiding the cold cuts (salami, rillettes, Parma ham) and rejecting the roast pork shoulder with honey and vinegar, savoring the chanterelles but discreetly pushing the *halouf* to the side of his plate without comment—the message was loud and clear, my aim being to find out all about the eating habits of each candidate—as usual Joseph and Sephora gobbled up whatever was set before them—no appetite this evening, Ismaël?—no, it's true, must be tired, and then I ate too much at lunch—I have to watch my weight!—but I spotted him gorging on cheese and hot apple tart, what an idiot!—wine flowed freely, jokes proliferated concerning God, the Belgians, the Swiss, but never really vulgar or dirty, all of which was perfect—when they all went off to shake their booties in the vaulted ballroom of the hotel's basement I settled down by the swimming pool to smoke a good cigar with the oldest of the assessors, Marc Bayol, a round little guy with glasses, calm, level-toned, an excellent psychologist, and share with him my by now mature thoughts on the candidates—we were agreed that Julien Lafarge, with his delayed adolescent's chubby cheeks, lacked the experience to be a leader of men—he was, in short, too young for the job—by contrast he considered Sephora well informed on technical matters but too detached, almost depressive, which was indeed quite possible—and he mistrusted Elsa Kaufmann, thought her too gifted, almost dangerous—Traoré and Abderhamane he was convinced by—I was tempted to ask him was he perhaps an anti-imperialist but opted to chew on my cigar under the starry sky and let the night bring its counsel.

The next morning I was out of luck: breakfast with Sephora of the sour armpits and Joseph the good Malian—Elsa was at another table in a black summer dress with broad white stripes that made her look ravishing, chatting with the three assessors—every day that passed her charm grew on me—wasn't very talkative with my tablemates, my imagination wandering over her form, got an instantaneous, serious hard-on—today would bring the greatest pressure to bear on our applicants—there was fatigue from the two previous days, plus very arduous tests in prospect—these included the individual presentations, the conflict-resolution exercise, and for the grand finale in late afternoon, the stress interview, which they did not expect, a surprise!

The presentations for each candidate dealt with food processing, legal issues, health standards, sanitary regulations, new dietetic ideas, agricultural suppliers—we were as interested in substance as in form, natch—they were all very competent—even Julien Lafarge managed to turn his presentation into what is known as "exciting drama"—it was just that I was irritated by a tic he had of continually adjusting his bow tie; might as well have been adjusting his balls, except that they were farther from his throat—Ismaël's presentation even made you want to ask questions, and Joseph's verbal skill was impressive: syntax very clear, rhythmic delivery, and an intense concentration that riveted the attention, bravo!—apart from her stranded-whale aspect, Sephora's diction was rather thick and her delivery monotonous—depressive, according to Marc Bayol.

By contrast all five contenders revealed serious shortcomings when it came to the conflict-resolution exercises—we worked with two scenarios: the employee adrift and the outraged customer, both parts played by the assessors, a thirty-minute high-anxiety test.

Joseph Traoré and Ismaël Abderhamane confirmed their inferiority complexes—Joseph turned despotic, a little Idi Amin throwing people to the crocodiles—Ismaël wavered, hesitant and too nice—Julien was incapable, simply *in-cap-ab-le*! of putting himself in the position of his interlocutor, he could not listen to anyone else—Sephora used and abused her authority like a Margaret Thatcher, wrinkling her nose as though her interlocutor suddenly stank of liquid manure—only Elsa survived unruffled—her nurse-cum-praying-mantis approach might have betrayed a wounding condescension to a paranoid, but her sheer charm got the poisoned pill swallowed and closed eyes to any whisper of offense—so for simple effectiveness Elsa carried the day, but of course . . .

We took lunch without the postulants in a private room so as to take stock for the first time—consensus quickly reached on the exclusion of Julien Lafarge, who decidedly still needed to grow up a bit—Sephora Aménidès, with her little rich girl's bulimia, was simply not presentable, as I pointed out a little brusquely in view of a certain hesitancy on the part of my directors—we are in food processing, for Christ's sake!—but what truly staggered me was the general good impression given by Joseph Traoré: true, he demonstrated real seriousness, seemed highly responsible, had a clear sense of duty—but you must be dreaming my fine friends if you think I'd hire a cannibal with a mouthful of teeth like the guy in the Banania ad—never, not for this company, at this level of responsibility! did you notice how his exotic colonial accent came on, yes-ma-fren-ah-bee-leeve-so, when he got hot and bothered in the conflict-resolution exercise?—no, no way—I don't need some black dancing naked in the rain when the harvest is good—besides, we're not selling coffee and peanuts here, goddammit! can you just picture him dealing with the agricultural co-ops? it's a culture clash, cassoulet and sauerkraut versus bunches of bananas! it's niet!—I was getting weird looks, so I made myself clear: this is not racism, just common sense about a natural incompatibility!—which left Ismaël and Elsa as the front-runners—the assessors found Elsa too manipulative—Brigitte was the most vehement; she spoke as a woman, she said: Elsa was devious, sly, insincere—it was the paradox of the actor, she concluded flatly—what? what's that you say? the paradox of what?—it's an essay by Diderot, she explained: maximum detachment of the actor, maximum effectiveness of his performance—everything artificial, calculated, measured in its effects—a cold-blooded reptile, absolutely no emotional investment, Elsa would never be loyal to the company spirit, or only long enough to build up a contact list, then decamp and start up a business of her own, perhaps even become a competitor, who knew?—I suspected that our Brigitte Charlay, well preserved at forty-something, a masterful woman, elegant, was entering menopause—she was jealous of Elsa—Marc Bayol had pointed out for his part that given Elsa's age, thirty-one, and her lack of children, she would soon, inevitably, confront us with a maternity leave problem—and if ever this Kaufmann woman were to drop two or three little ones, we would merely be financing the creation of a family—hardly a profitable activity, wouldn't I say, for such an important position?—and what about Ismaël Abderhamane?—they all agreed, he was the perfect social lubricator, with a well-nigh instinctive ability to connect—attentive to the other person, responsible, brilliant! a true man of harmony, able to make others assume responsibility and inspire everyone—and he's cute too, put in Brigitte, which does no harm!—I turned to Bayol—just look at the whole person: this is a mature man, father of three children, stable family situation, and a frantic desire to assimilate, probably inherited from his parents—in other words, a diehard loyalty will be yours! to my mind this is your production manager!—I nodded with the pensive air of a monarch considering the pleas of his vassals, the flame of profound reflection burning deep in his gray cells—we still have the stress interview, I concluded, let's leave things open till tonight.

Lunch over, we rejoined our five applicants at a table close to the swimming pool and tried to get their measure in another way by inviting them to play eight holes of golf—Sephora made the excuse that she did not have her outfit, etc.—so much the better, she was liable to hack up the green if not injure someone with her club—Julien pleaded several telephone appointments, Abderhamane his notes to go over before the final test—Traoré was sweating, embarrassed, the only one to admit to me that he didn't play and would be unable to so much as putt the ball—Elsa got to her feet, accepted the invitation, and asked for a few minutes to change—my God! how beautiful she was in that dress!—golf bespeaks breeding, status, social background, and merely suggesting half a round was a trial in itself—Elsa had perfectly grasped what was at stake—she was the one to have brought her togs and clubs, aware of what kind of hotel had been chosen for the recruitment seminar—I waited for her in the lobby until she came tripping down the stairs in two-toned golf shoes, a white cotton outfit, very masculine except for the green patch of a silk pocket, her clubs in a soft leather bag—she had her hair in a chignon, she was smiling, and here we were strolling on the course, over the grass—her bearing so elegant and discreet that it obliged me to mind my manners—she said little, replying elliptically to my questions about her childhood, her parents, the place where she grew up—she was focused, perfectionist, able, could hardly be reproached for taking her game so seriously, so much so in fact that she was going to win if I didn't stop looking at her instead of examining the terrain and considering my tactics—I'm a very poor player, never give up so long as I have the slightest chance of reversing the score, can't stand losing—Elsa! if you get the better of me, you can forget about the position!—she smiled, took her last hole in three masterful strokes, her motions fluid, economical, powerful—how magnificent the curve of her back as she struck the ball, and calves to dream on! and there it was—she had won and I was not even put out! such a long time since any woman had taken my breath away like this! so, Mr. Windel, I guess it's game over for me?—my dear Elsa, yes, you are in big trouble—you should have stayed chatting with your colleagues by the pool—she sighed—our fates depend on such little things, don't they?—yes indeed, by a thread, and never the thread you think!—my God! it's five past six! we'd better hurry! are you . . . are you going to keep your victory outfit on?—no, I was planning to change, take a shower, and—well, if I may make so bold, your dress of this morning suited you perfectly!—why, thank you, I'll bear that in mind, Mr. Windel—my God in heaven! I swore I'd take her on my boat to the Red Sea the next month! my prick was standing up like a pikestaff.

Apart from Elsa, who was changing, we were soon all gathered for the last lap—the last interview, my friends—you're wiped out, I know;

be Zen, no tears and no fighting allowed!—smiles all round—come on, it's true!—the thing was to reduce the tension in the air, melt the frostiness that tends to form just before the final judgment—breathe deeply everyone, and be nice, Rome is watching you! summing up and results to come just before dinner.

This is the kind of interview that I almost revel in, maximum intensity, the art of navigation in a Category 8 hurricane. You put the candidate under pressure by means of unwelcome allusions and provocative questions, you play on his or her nerves—you remain on your feet, circling him or her like vultures, then suddenly, out of the blue, you go on the attack: we have strong doubts, you know, about your ability to meet the requirements of the position—at which Sephora paled—you . . . have you seen my CV?—we've been together here for three days—yes, Sephora, that's just it—what do you mean? I know food processing, without pretension or fanfare, it's my field!—eight years I've been working in it, networks, flow charts, professional codes and practices, costings, people, markets, Europe-wide! what do you want? should I get naked and dance the Waikiki hula with ostrich plumes stuck up my ass?—no, Sephora, I interjected, I think not!—it's true you're well acquainted with food processing, but you're very badly acquainted with its dietetic aspect—she was no longer pale, she was livid—fuck you, you bastard! your food has nothing dietetic about it!—and bang! she slammed the door—goodbye Sephora! one less place setting for the closing dinner!—I warned you, Mr. Windel, she's depressed—we are not a psychiatric clinic here, I retorted—next!—ah, Julien, come on in, my dear fellow—no, don't sit down, we stand for this interview—you may walk about, up and down, before you answer—he smiled—your knowledge of financial matters is impressive, but your actual liking for food seems very hands-off—but no, not at all! I have lots of ideas about the creation of new quality products, and—here we went! he was going to rehearse the future for us, à la Jérôme Guichard—my taste in foods is not confined to cassoulet, split peas, and sauer-kraut—you're forgetting garden peas and carrots—well, yes, but that's much the same—we have doubts, Julien, about your ability to commit yourself to a position like this—why? is it my age that puts you off?—possibly; this would be only your second job and—but Julien Lafarge did not back down, kept arguing to the bitter end that he was the right person—his grit was an agreeable surprise to us—even though he was not about to become Guichard's successor, he needed to be encouraged—we would provide him with a detailed report on his test performance so that he could avoid making the same mistakes again—let him come and see us in five years' time!—Mr. Traoré, do come in! blue-gray double-breasted suit, impeccable, could easily picture him as a UN diplomat—we began with elaborate compliments, getting him off his guard, and then, without his getting the slightest hint of the attack: but isn't this position too high for you after all? he stopped dead, in full flight, like a duck receiving a bellyful of lead just as it climbs into a purple wetlands sky—he blanched, if I may be forgiven this highly inappropriate description of his ebony countenance—long silence, drooping shoulders, then the collapse, the inferiority complex itself seeming to speak its name—yes, you're right—don't have what it takes, need to be humble, as my father said, either obtain a position higher than my present one or . . . or else I should take orders—what was that? I beg your pardon—yes, I was going to get ordained—my place is most likely among the poor, with my brothers—my legal and financial knowledge would perhaps be useful there—why don't you look into the IMF or the Bank of West African States? asked Brigitte Charlay—you are telling me that this position here is too high-level for me, so how could I possibly obtain one at the Bank of African States?—why, Mr. Traoré, thanks to your seriousness and your motivation! said Marc Bayol, piling on—thank you for your advice; I shall read your conclusions with great interest—may I leave you now?—certainly, Mr. Traoré, if you wish—a dead silence followed his exit, a sense of discomfort—strange that he should melt down like that, but it shows that the job is not for him, wouldn't you say, my dear colleagues?—at first, when Elsa appeared, I was disappointed, irritated, indeed bitterly resentful toward her—she had in fact put on a different dress, yellow, pleated, waisted, with a square neckline barely hiding the rising slope of her breasts—she was defying me, the little devil—true, she looked dazzling—my anger melted like snow in the sunshine, rushing away like a mountain torrent, and eventually it was all bravo, Elsa!—come on, everyone, get out of here! get out I say!! I have a boner! a boner! jump on her, tumble her over a desk, or even on the floor—confusedly, I heard the interview beginning—the assessors did not want her, my directors were neutral, the personal attack on her was intense: should you not fear, Brigitte Charlay wanted to know, that, as in the past, you won't be up to the responsibility?—Elsa did not give an inch, calmly explaining how she had always been up to her responsibilities, including those that were hers at present—we think, broke in Bayol, that your capacities simply do not meet the requirements of this position—she showed that this was questionable by presenting her own summary of three days of perfect clarity and correctness, slipping in the afterthought that she (like the others for that matter) would hardly have reached this stage of the recruitment seminar if we really thought she was incompetent—bam! put that in your pipe and smoke it!—all the while smiling, amiable—with her devastating charm, she won if not the admiration then at least the respect of the assessors—thank you, Mademoiselle Kaufmann, we'll be seeing you shortly—she closed the door gently behind her, stupefaction in the assembled company—we looked from one to the other until Bayol, with a wry pout, exclaimed: she's deadly, that girl, perfectly deadly—but my dear Marc, she's innocent, surely, until proven guilty, this Elsa Kaufmann has calmly played the game these last three days, and she was selected by your agency as one of the five best applicants, and that after your first round of telephone interviews, I simply don't understand your misgivings!—my human-resources director and my sales director nodded, seemingly in agreement with me at last—what a pair of pantywaists, perfectly insensitive to Elsa's voluptuous magnetism!—come in, Ismaël, come on in! no, we don't sit down, we walk around the room freely—in a circle or a square? he asked—a sharp sense of humor, this Ismaël, a master of the art of sociability, as my colleagues would say—our group spontaneously adopted a tactic similar to the one used on Joseph Traoré—first put him at ease, hinting at the great fund of goodwill we had for him personally and pitching him soft questions: what is your conception of a higher middle manager? how far would your devotion to your company go? what would its limits be? and what about your private life, your family life? how would you balance your obligations on the two fronts? etc.—his replies were perfect! just what we wanted!—splendid, Ismaël! you covered all the angles! splendid!—then I went on the attack: tell me though, Ismaël, there's one thing that nags at me—as you know, as well as anyone I'm sure, we manufacture, or rather we prepare cassoulet, lentils, sauerkraut, split peas—yes, and green peas and carrots also—okay, my friend, keep on grinning while you can; it won't last long!—yes, indeed, but . . . but in every case the base, the foundation, the theme of our prepared dishes is shoulder of pork, pig's knuckles, pork sausage, pork belly—in short, all meats coming from, ah, the pig—so don't you have any doubts at all about concerning yourself continually with meat of this kind?—I sensed that I had pulled him up short in the middle of his one-man show—he had shifted instantaneously to thirty-six frames per second, serious slow motion—we gathered around him, not a perfect circle but all focused on his person, suddenly, oppressively, awaiting his answer, we wanted an answer!—he knew it, turned pale—no, no, he answered, hesitating—I don't understand the question—I set him straight: your religion forbids you to eat *halouf*, does it not?—but Mr. Windel, I'm not religious, I am secular and Republican! in any case religion is a private matter, and—of course, of course, but forgive me for insisting, in this instance you'll have to deal with the suppliers, visit them, check and assess the quality of their products, their kitchens' output, sample the dishes as called for, be able to appreciate a good pork shoulder, for example, and—no problem, Mr. Windel, I'm a gourmet, and

my palate, you might say, is like . . . like a CAT scanner!—which
drew a smile from us—all the same, during our dinners together I
got the feeling that you were systematically leaving any pork on the
side of your plate—am I mistaken?—I could tell that our Ismaël
was cornered, dry mouth, sticky tongue—well, that evening I wasn't
hungry, I suppose, and—come, come, Mr. Abderhamane, please be
honest with us—it's true, I was raised to reject *halouf*, but for a
company that becomes my body and soul—you got *that* right, yes,
that's just it!—I . . . I can deal with pork, taste it if need be, and—but
it will taste disgusting, surely? how can you be sure? how can you
give instructions to the suppliers, their cooks? how will you be cred-
ible? you can never draw on a long experience of the flavor of *halouf*!
and as for singing its praises, I just can't imagine it!—but this is a
job, Mr. Windel, I can commit myself to it—yes, right, body and
soul!—everyone had closed in on him, agog, watching his Adam's
apple going up and down like a yo-yo—the three assessors were
surrounding him as though they wanted to support him, protect
him, encourage him, get him out of trouble—at this point I made
my way into the little group and made the old-faithful observation
that never fails to stress out the candidate on the spot: the fact is,
we strongly doubt your ability to meet the requirements of the
position!—and simultaneously, indeed with perfect synchronicity,
I released a silent, tepid, dense fart, a pestilential emission, a
quasi-toxic gas slowly permeating our company—ah! flatulence-
tympanites-meteorism! gas as the invisible weapon, as the most
destructive of weapons—this message from the viscera soon reached
our olfactory senses, nostrils wrinkled, the air became noxious—it
was the fart of a convict on a steady diet of lousy beans, and it
occurred to me, by the bye, that here was a market segment we had
not yet targeted for our lower-end offerings: the central purchasing
offices of the penal system!—schools and retirement communities,
we had those pretty well covered, but not the prisons!—anyway!—what
pig was it that farted? was the question in every nose and on every
lip of our learned assembly, and since everyone had their attention

fixed at that moment firmly on Abderhamane, eager to see how he would react to the disobliging comment made to him ten seconds earlier, he concluded (correctly, in fact!) that blame for the odor had fallen on him, was now the monkey on his back—it made sense of course: the emotion, the anxiety had taken hold of him, and he had let out a memorable stinker at the perfect moment—there, that was his reply, the body speaking while the mouth kept silent—he was not just off balance now, Ismaël, he was waxen, transformed into a paranoid North African amid rich, dominant, white Christians who ate *halouf* and *tolerated* him—his history had caught up with him in the worst way—he was stammering something about his good faith, poor Ismaël, and faith was indeed it. Exit Abderhamane.

11

Escalation

And she slapped him with all her might: answer! admit it! react!—she
slapped him again—he got up, the Bulgarian-style yogurt in his left
hand, and threw it in her face—she reciprocated immediately—the
two of them now with face, hair, chest streaked with yogurt, she closed
her fist, and bonk! punched him in the nose, broke his glasses, a
splinter lodging in his left eyebrow—he slapped her in turn with the
fury of a condemned man—they were both bleeding, blood running
over their lips, dripping from their chins like strawberry milk—she
grabbed the hot skillet from the stove, in it a few sarladaise potatoes
cooling in goose fat, garlic, and parsley, and taking the handle in both
hands, a club, she brought it down like an axe on his skull, a great
crack of shattering wood, the wood of the handle still in her grip,
his scalp ripped open, blood zigzagging across his receding hairline,
he seizing an Opinel knife from the table, she wheeling quickly
back to the stove, this time getting hold of the heavy perforated
chestnut-roasting pan, handle and pan both of metal—the two of
them panting now, running out of breath, nostrils dilated, ashen,

two gladiators, she with her bludgeon, he with his blade, she backed away into the hallway and toward the staircase, he followed her, they sized each other up, watching for the precise moment to attack, the microsecond of opportunity in which to down the opponent—she climbed the stairs backward, reached the two-thirds mark—now! he decided that it was now! before the turn, the bend in the stairs, and he bounded forward, Spartacus!—knife pointing forward, he missed a step, almost fell flat at her feet, which were shod in black ballerinas with blue pompoms—she took advantage of this and swung her chestnut pan like a golf club—his bloodied head snapped back, bending his body out into the empty space of the stairwell, his demolished face stamped by roughly circular patches conforming to the pattern of holes in the bottom of the pan—he swayed back and forth for a second, two seconds, then toppled over and spiraled head over heels all the way down, the knife entering his chest, and lay senseless, losing blood, at the bottom of the stairs, my father as stricken hero—she dropped the pan in a glacial silence, raced down toward him, sick with dread, her legs trembling, overbalanced, collapsed on top of his body, in the process driving the knife in up to the hilt and into his aorta, slitting it neatly!—convulsive little coughs brought blood to his lips, oozing out and forming sticky plaques on the tiled floor of the hallway, and she shaking him as though he were sleeping—"no time even to buy more teaspoons," he croaked, the words overtaken by his last gasp—a vague smile, then two minutes later his last shudders—she was sentenced to twenty years of imprisonment, twelve of them without parole—she would not plead guilty, which only increased her prison term—her eyes still shooting daggers of vengeful hatred, she merely declared, proudly, insolently: I shall be a worthy widow!

Found myself in an orphanage after three fine years with Grandma Blanche, the one who always maintained that it was not a chestnut pan but a grill pan—no! I insisted, immovable, I was right there until his last words!—yes, but you were too little!—you are wrong, Gran, your memory is good at six and three-quarters!—in fact it was my fault; I should have cleared the table, put the utensils away, pans, knives, forks—should have intervened, thrown myself between them, arms wide, shouting at the top of my lungs: stop! the war is over! at the moment when my father had his head in his hands—but their bodies, their voices, their looks exercised such a primal force that I was petrified—they were giants; it was a battle of titans two and a half times my size.

It's true, though, they never got on; their way of being together was fighting, all very ordinary of course—and then there was the scene that lasted several weeks, a veritable Olympiad of contention, over some silver dessert spoons that he was supposed to clean at the factory where he worked, and where he had access to electrolytic materials, or something like that—the little spoons would have come back shining like new! eleven of them altogether, and in short he lost them at his workshop, spoons that had come down to her from her parents, the father and mother that she worshipped with an almost mystical love—she harried him every day God sent when he got back from work, until he finally admitted (bad mistake!) that he had lost them—they were likely pinched by a workmate—he was trapped now, couldn't wriggle out of it: no more without fail dear I'll take care of them tomorrow dear! no, this time he was up against the wall—and then came the ground swell, vindictive, over his unconsciousness, indifference, egoism, incompetence, chronic absentmindedness, stupid naivety, blind cruelty: sarcastic remarks, insults, humiliations—he bore them in silence for long days, devastated by his error of judgment: to have left such a treasure kicking about on his workbench, such a prize in full view of the covetous eyes of people who could barely make ends meet—what idiocy! until one day he raised his head, rebelled against her relentlessness, as if his error were fatal, as if the opprobrium and dishonor were to be passed on down the generations, like the vendetta between the two families, a reference to her Corsican heritage—and now he would shout louder than her, declaring his exhaustion, his helplessness, and proposing divorce—ah! that's so easy! now that you've squandered my inheritance!—they were forever going up and down the stairs that led from the kitchen/dining room/hallway/toilet to the bedrooms/bathroom of the single upper floor, doors slammed, rage and hatred filled the air, a weird place-changing ballet: ground floor to second floor, second floor to ground floor, no passing on the staircase, where one might jostle the other—then at last, both of them worn out, out of arguments, vocal cords raw, they ceased reviling each other—a leaden silence, a kind of curfew, descended upon the house for at most a week, until at meals they began once more to ask for the salt, the water, a piece of bread, and to evoke the weather forecast, say how tiring the day was, he for his part carefully eschewing the words "factory," "workshop," or "workbench"—but fate was lurking like a starving wolf when, with the Bulgarian yogurt before them, that evening in May, she asked him to get teaspoons from the table drawer on his side—he hastened to oblige—too hasty! his feverish and clumsy gesture caused the spoons to fall on the kitchen's tiled floor—reaching to pick them up, she spotted the twelfth dessert spoon, the one she had thought lost from the silver set of her deceased, late lamented parents, and now the only one! the one and only spoon of the service still in her possession—tears filled her eyes as though flowing, surging forth from some water table of unfinished mourning—you bastard! you stinking bastard! how could you have been so oblivious, so unconscious, so disrespectful of the memory of my family! I have so little left of theirs! they were so poor and miserable, just janitors in a tiny janitor's flat—my mother's younger sister stole everything, taking advantage of his death, which devastated her, the elder sister—why, she was prostrate with sorrow!—and you, you'll be the death of me!—he had his elbows on the table, and it was then that he took his head in his hands, and I heard him mutter: my God, not this all life long?

12

Face?

True, we had all overdone it with the blow, with joints as fat as cucumbers, and in the cabin we were very seriously ripped, already in the wide blue yonder . . . but on the ground, earlier, we had been clean, straight, planning the flight, readying the parachute gear; everything was thoroughly checked . . . there was a wait for a while before takeoff for the wind to drop, a cameraman from regional France 3 TV was with us, along to film us in free fall, we were supposed to create beautiful group formations . . . a long-drawn-out hour on the ground chatting and smoking dope in a hangar, sitting on pallets, with this Laurent guy from France 3, he had a big Betacam on his knees and had already done several stories on skydiving. We had no retired military types, just us, happy at the prospect of hurling ourselves into thin air at three thousand meters and combining our bird-like bodies into a variety of configurations as residues of hash and grass coursed through our super-oxygenated brains; we would soon be leaving for the far reaches of interstellar space . . . some of the gang, the craziest, would go up in helicopters, jump out with skis fixed, and glide calmly over high mountaintops before sloughing off their parachutes two meters above the ground and beginning oh-wow slides down slopes of mind-boggling steepness, descents into virgin, immaculate powder . . . they called it a "total snow" experience: snow up the nose, snow from head to foot, absolute whiteness! . . . anyway, we eventually piled into the cabin of our plane and crammed ourselves onto uncomfortable benches, frequently overcome by spasms of laughter, slipping onto the floor with our parachutes on our backs and kneeling there, doubled over with mirth and, in short, hardly models of equilibrium, but certain that, once poised high in the blue, we would easily retrieve our birdman moves . . . once in the drop zone we were to jump the seven of us, and Laurent would follow forty seconds later (the time it took the Cessna to loop back to the zone) so as to film us from above, looking down at us with the mountains as backdrop. Ready! set! go, go, go! wow! the bay was open, and amid the familiar racket created by wind and props we leaped into the sky singing about the seven dwarfs going off to work, passed quickly through the last layer of audible engine noise, and at last, thirty meters farther down, entered pure, infinite silence, suspension-dilation-extension: if God exists it is at that instant, that very instant, as heart-stopping as soul and flesh can bear, a fragment of eternity . . . soon you notice a barely perceptible lapping sound, the sound of clothes snapping in the air ruffled by our descent, then you come to, 150 meters down now, and already hand in hand we are forming the great ring of the origins, our faces wreathed in marveling smiles . . . at the two-hundred-meter mark we go into our celestial/geometrical formation cycle . . . the physical principle is simple: against the centrifugal pull, stay in contact with your partners, taking hold one by one and reciprocally of wrists and ankles, each of our bodies a link in the web that keeps us fast together, a web that we cling to in order to move as a unit and morph internally into line/circle/square/triangle/star, completing a formation never quite so exhilarating as breaking up to assemble another . . . and it is our mere bodies that create a rickety mooring, an immaterial terra firma, a platform floating in the ether without set shape or structure . . . but enough of the lyrical skydiver mysticism . . . despite the general euphoria, our choreography was now unfolding in meticulously controlled sequences rehearsed a thousand times on the ground, Laurent was a hundred meters above us filming the ballet, all was for the best in this corner of paradise, until the moment when our wrist altimeters decreed that the time had come to separate and open chutes—there were one thousand meters to go when I heard André on my left screaming: open! Laurent! open! what are you waiting for? open! . . . but our cameraman was dropping like a stone a few dozen meters from us, his legs mimicking a kind of convulsive walk, trying desperately to straighten up his head and shoulders—you could see that he wanted to keep his balance and remain perpendicular, but he plummeted toward the ground as if drawn helplessly into a chasm, his eye riveted to his camera and his camera pointed at the earth racing to meet him . . . open! for Christ's sake! open! . . . there is nothing to open, André! Laurent had jumped from the aircraft without a chute, just his camera harness; he must have put his pack down at some point in the cabin, who knows why . . . and not one of us, stoned as we were, falling about, yucking it up, doubled up like hunchbacks, noticed a thing, and we had jumped like a bunch of kids leaping into a swimming pool . . . Laurent was still in free fall before our eyes; we were stuck to the sky like butterflies in a glass case, watching him get farther and farther away as he plunged to his fate . . . he went on filming, as though seeking refuge in his viewfinder, in the image of death traveling toward him, death in the garb of spring-fresh grass specked with flowers, with crocuses, on the lower slopes of mountain pastureland—perhaps he thought that projecting his whole body into the cinematic frame of the fast-approaching earth would save him from being crushed, perhaps he was filming so as not to fall for lack of support, so as not to hurtle out of his hallucinated view into the ground now springing up at him, and he went on filming until the impact: a patch of flesh, bone, and blood awaited us now below our feet, no more grass or flowers but a landing-ground of blood after a slow, asphyxiating return to find death a fait accompli. His film would be shown not on regional France 3 but instead on all the eight o'clock newscasts, homage to a colleague killed on the job, filming till the bitter end, a Molière dying onstage . . .

And that was where I did not understand this sudden explosion of rage, its vehemence shocking and dumbfounding me—I refer to the reaction of a friend, a few days later, who as I was recounting the fateful incident suddenly broke in, peremptory, virulent, brutal: so slapdash! so half-assed of him! what the fuck do you want with a forty-second shot of a grassy field coming up at you? it wasn't the ground he should have shot, you can get that by dropping a camera from the air—it was himself, his face, his expression, the look in his eyes, as he slammed through the air, knowing he was going to die, the cinematic work of his life the living face of a man falling, and waiting . . . but by filming this futile anecdotal footage he wasted his death, he wasted it! I was overwhelmed, stunned, stammering: but Michel, how can you be so uncompromisingly for life? . . . what you ask is monstrous and—he contemplated me tenderly, sadly: do we have a choice?

14

Dodging

He came whining to my office—must have judged it better to appeal to the human resources department than to his saints!—on account of his worksite accident I made an exception and, yes, in the end agreed to see him—but this was an exception, absolutely an exception!—they weren't going to turn my seventy-square-meter corner office, with its view onto the Quai de Seine, into a consolation center, handkerchiefs and antidepressants free on demand! there would be a zigzag queue at my door in no time, and fifty-odd supplicants already packed into my vital space—I'd be like Napoleon visiting plague victims during the Egyptian Campaign—and "whining" is putting it mildly—what de Souza needed was a health summary to be drawn up six weeks after his surgery—but naturally the wretched man brought not a single document—no post-op write-up, no prescription for physical therapy, no medical certificate, no unfit-for-work note, nothing! paperwork was not his forte; it scared him—he probably couldn't read or write, at least not in French and I daresay not in Portuguese either; in fact he had been desperately demanding a literacy course for three years now—unfortunately for him he was a first-rate mason, the indispensable sort, and he could never be spared long enough to free up time for language lessons.

When my secretary opened the door for him, I watched him drag himself in on his two crutches, with his sideshow-wrestler's build, like a slug balancing on a tightrope—my dear Manuel! delighted to see you! on your way to complete recovery, I trust?!—we need you, do your realize that?—oh, Monsieur Duschesne, I'm allowed off my crutches starting next week, the surgeon says so!—so you see, etc.—in short, two minutes of friendly words and expressions of concern, the children, the family, is everyone well? blah, blah, blah—then we got down to cases—you come to me without a single document, Monsieur de Souza, with your hands in your pockets! that just won't do!—I'm sorry, Monsieur Duchesne, I didn't think, was so happy to get out, come here, visit you at headquarters, didn't think at all about doctor's notes, Social Security papers—didn't think! didn't think! Mister Didn't-Think! his *u*'s were pronounced like *oo*'s, "esscoozay-moi, ploo doo too pensé à la Sécooritay Zos-siale"—the accent irritates me, never got used to it in my fifteen-year career, and lord knows I've run into enough Portuguese/Spanish on BTP's construction sites! still, let's not complain, they are great workers—and the last six years, with the malignant spread of Africans on the sites—another kettle of fish entirely, and more complicated, even if they pronounce their *u*'s perfectly—you'll just have to come back with your complete medical file, Monsieur de Souza—would you take care of it with my secretary please? she'll pass your paperwork to my assistant, he'll be doing the follow-up on you—look after yourself, regards to your family—Board of Directors meeting in twenty minutes, two files to review before that, and oh! I was forgetting: Alvarez, site manager on the Canal Plus building, was going to meet his Waterloo—absenteeism, insults to the architects, embezzlement from the slush fund, a mountain of dough on a site of this size! I'm talking about the slush fund, fed by the customary kickbacks from suppliers, that serves to pay for on-site celebrations of birthdays, weddings, births, and funerals, to provide bonuses off the books, to make payments under the table, and to subsidize the big bash when the job is finished, a major event for workers who have been together for six months or a year building a twenty-story tower, for example—for every new project all the work teams are reshuffled, a real jigsaw puzzle, but the main thing is to break up work groups—they create bonds that are too firm, solidarities—it's repugnant! people start thinking that they should unionize, wanting to stick their noses in planning management, construction specifications, security issues—wanting to develop an esprit de corps—such shit!—well, we get it, we hear you loud and clear! five by five!

One construction site equals one team—then it's back to square one, every time, every part is reassigned, that way we get rid of the bullshit artists—they are dispersed, atomized, sent off, say, to build an extension to the A6 autoroute, and that's that! when even so much as a couple gets together around here, even if the two of them work in different sections, bang! one of them has to quit the ship, that's the house rule, you can take it from me! the danger is any bonding, any lateral connections—all relations must be vertical! partitioned! individuals and sections must be partitioned off! we are a great and beautiful community, all pulling together to conquer markets, but! each person is alone! one for all, yes! all for one, no! it's a question of hygiene, as old Francis Bouygues whispered before handing the reins to his sons and heirs. Right now, a decision had to be made about replacing Alvarez, easing him out discreetly—and, lucky me, Manuel de Souza had taken only five minutes of my time!

Three weeks went by, then, coming out of a meeting, I bumped into the aforesaid Manuel de Souza, wringing his cap and palavering with Sylvie, my secretary—hello there, Monsieur de Souza, is all going well? no more crutches, I notice! back to work soon, I suppose—you have all your paperwork?—Sylvie nodded, but I sensed that she was stricken—oh, Monsieur Duchesne, it's true, I'm walking on my two legs, as you see—that doesn't surprise me, knowing you, Manuel, you have a will of iron—but there's a big problem, Monsieur Duchesne, oh yes, the surgeon told me: both your heels are fixed, you can walk carefully on them, in sneakers, but no more construction sites for you—heavy lifting, pushing wheelbarrows full of cement, climbing ladders, I've been declared unfit for those—but you haven't returned to normal yet! all that is only temporary, Monsieur de Souza!—sorry, Monsieur Duchesne, it's the last thing I want, you know, but this is definitive; they can't make any more repairs—I could feel his face, his body wilting, the anxiety, the panic gripping his insides—he couldn't do anything else, and as for us, I wondered what we were going to do with this Manuel; we couldn't keep him on—what a shitty situation—and anyway, whatever possessed him to bust himself up falling off a ladder? the idiot slid down the whole length of it, six meters no less, reduced his heels to mush in his safety boots—he had just been promoted to foreman too, he was happy, we couldn't put his literacy training off any longer—that was a genuine obsession of his, though I must confess I didn't get it: with his hands ravaged by cement, his fingers plumped up like Strasburg sausages, how could he even hold a pen? it's wild the crazy notions some people come up with—and a foreman has precious little writing to do, but still, this time we had agreed to his starting the course when the job ended in November—but now it was goodbye calf, cow, pig, and chicks—no more promotion, no more literacy course, just dismissal with a severance bonus and an 18 percent disability pension!—no longer our responsibility or our shekels! tough to say, it was up to him to sort himself out with the insurance and the disability people—ah, Monsieur de Souza, this is all very difficult!—yes, Monsieur Duchesne, that's just what I was saying to Madame Denizeau, I . . . could I start my classes right now?—yes, I mean the language courses, and then we could see later about my reclassification—I'd be more skilled, have more possibilities (ploo d'opportoonités, c'est soor!)—because I don't want to leave the company, it's my home here, eighteen years I've been working here—I . . . I can't give you a reply right away, off the cuff, Monsieur de Souza—we'll have to think it over, but don't worry, we'll find a solution—let's say we'll let you know our decision at the beginning of next month, okay? in any case no time is being lost; you are on sick leave until then—I must leave you now, there's a truckload of work on my desk—sad to say, the fact was that we could offer him nothing—de Souza was screwed—which reminded me, I had to chew Sylvie out—she mustn't pull that sort of fake funereal face in front of an employee because she assumes (correctly!) that it's curtains for him—she'll only upset him, make him suspect the worst, get his defenses up, and at the end of the day drive him to the ombudsman! no! no! you have to smile, lull him with the prospect of an internal deal, a happy outcome, and then let him go with expressions of regret, respect, and contrition, making him appreciate how generous our severance package is—this was a pisser: she ought to have known better after all this time, an elementary rule of personnel management—she would be bumped down to the mailroom or to reception and telephone answering if she didn't shape up! Christ! I'd told her already! a hundred times! this Mother Teresa stuff, shit! let her fuck off and do charity work in Ethiopia, or in Darfur, to hell with her!—there, now I was in a filthy temper; she had ruined my morning!

Two weeks later de Souza's file was filed, his case closed, we tried to find him a niche, every slot was filled—his lay-off notice was signed and sealed, the terms of his severance package settled with the approval of our team of employment lawyers—I was in the field on the site of the new Bobigny prefecture, completion deadline the end of 2007, for an inspection with the site manager, Fosco—we were standing beneath the north façade with the four foremen, the team leaders, all in hardhats and work boots—we had a tense situation, conflict over the allotment of responsibilities; a fight had almost ended badly two days before on the eighth raw-concrete deck, arbitration required! Carlos Fosco was overwhelmed—the discussion was brief and bitter; I calmed things down, made proposals that seemed to suit everyone, promised to come back the following week, we all shook hands—shit! shit! shit! what is that one doing here?—was I talking to him, Fosco wanted to know—yes, Fosco, you're the boss on this site, at least for now! what is Manuel de Souza doing here? he's meant to be gone!—he . . . he came to enjoy the atmosphere of the worksite, see his comrades—comrades? comrades? I take it, Fosco, that you mean his colleagues?—yes, yes, his colleagues—yes, that's more like it—when I thought that his severance was going out the next day by registered mail it pissed me off to run into him here—good day, Monsieur Duchesne; so, are you on an inspection tour?—good day, Manuel, how are you? you seem, er, frisky!?—I mean you seem solid, in the pink!—he had a red hardhat, but apart from that he was wearing an ugly beige smock over a blue checked shirt and fluorescent mauve-green sneakers with thick soles and little compressed-air-filled heels with springs—you are like a young man, I offered—he smiled, but a worry line creased his forehead—are you here visiting your colleagues? checking the progress on the site, I suppose? and what does your expert eye tell you, Manuel?—well, Monsieur Duchesne, everything seems to be going well, all is in order, but without safety boots, as you know, I'm not allowed up on the decks; I can only get a general impression—you . . . have you decided about me? the beginning of next month is tomorrow, and—I didn't know what to say, so I blustered, made stuff up, anything: oh yes, Monsieur de Souza, we're working on that, we're having a meeting a bit later to talk things over calmly, and—do you think I can start my course straightaway?—I can't promise you anything, it's not a done deal—but, then?—Fosco had moved away discreetly, he got it, and we were alone—I was mussing my black oxfords, they were covered by a layer of dust—hard to be well turned out on a worksite!—and this guy, at the prefecture's north façade no less, what rotten luck!—why did I have to run into him here! a sort of mean silence grew between the two of us, all you could hear were cement mixers and cranes, then all of a sudden, with Herculean force, he flung his arms around my waist, shoved me along, and threw me to the ground about five meters farther on, almost falling on top of me, as though (I thought to myself) possessed by a sudden fury and a terrifying strength—he had blown a fuse, taken leave of his senses, and in a split second decided to do me in!—but then a deafening crash accompanied by a dull rumble rose from the ground, which shook, and we were splattered by liquid concrete, shrouded in dust—like a bomb going off! a bomb deflagrating, in the shape of a closed loading funnel filled with half a metric ton of concrete fallen from the tenth deck and exploded, volatilized, strewn far and wide—the point of impact the very same, identical, perfectly targeted spot where we were talking, now more or less a crater, and had not Manuel de Souza tackled me to the ground like a rugby player we would now be chopped meat in a bath of concrete—are you okay? okay?—shouts and exclamations could be heard, people racing toward us from all sides—you . . . you saved my life, Manuel, thank you, thank you! I thank you for that! shit! death was at our heels, just three seconds away!—we got to our feet, streaked with dust, clothes and faces dripping with liquid concrete—Fosco came up with a foreman and three laborers, and dozens of hardhats poked out from every deck, staring down at us—listen, Manuel, just tell me, I sincerely want to know why for Christ's sake you are so obsessed with taking that goddamned literacy course, I just don't get it!—but, Monsieur Duchesne, it's for my two boys who are just going to their big school, and it's difficult! I want to help them with their homework, so they write properly, read properly! being a mason, frankly, is too hard!—oh, so that's it, okay, okay—couldn't finish my sentence; they were all around us, all wanting to know were we in one piece—isn't that obvious? I retorted witheringly—they were all white-faced; we were clowns with gray facial masks wandering about a building—fuck it, Fosco! this sort of thing happens every five years! I want a report from the chief security officer on my desk in two hours! I mean a frigging detailed report on the causes of this foul-up! and in my humble opinion his goose was cooked; as of tonight he could clear out!—okay, enough time wasted! I asked for overalls, meaning to go home, wash up, get into another suit, then return to the office on Quai de Seine—shit!

what a day!—Fosco steered me toward the prefabricated shed where tools, clothing, hardhats, and boots were stored—oh, just a minute—I shook Manuel's hand again, addressed him effusively: goodbye, Monsieur de Souza, and let me thank you once more, I insist, most sincerely—oh yes, I, uh—it's not definite yet—as I was telling you, can't promise anything, but we're discussing it later at the meeting, I'll keep you informed, good evening!—I made my escape, totally stressed, nerves jangling as though electrified, took a few steps, at which point Fosco was inspired to add: de Souza, all the same, good job he did there, saved your life, that's a fact—well, yes, I grumbled, and it's a pity—tell me, Fosco, who is he, for pete's sake, the site security manager? what's his name?

15

Airbag

Not guilty! not guilty! I remember the transports of joy, of relief—my
Jennifer, her golden mane flowing over her shoulders, her leopard-
skin jacket, a thousand points of light cast off by the diamonds on
her delightful earlobes, racing into my arms, perching on her stiletto
heels, and yes, with her right hand, an emerald on the middle finger
and a ruby on the ring finger, starting to fondle my male member, an
instant hard-on—but sweetheart! shit! her elephant-hide bracelet
with its 70-carat clip was catching on my alpaca pants, pulling on a
thread—stop it, for Christ's sake! we're in a courtroom! the victim's
parents are here, collapsed on a bench, sobbing!—my lawyers were
congratulating me, the one from the insurance and the one paid out
of my bank account—it's I who should congratulate you, gentlemen,
drinks at my place, champagne and petits fours!—I waved vaguely
at the stricken parents, had an urge to go over and shake hands
with them—no hard feelings, okay?—but five steps from them I
froze—time to hop it! we fled the court, climbed into Jennifer's red
Austin Cooper S, Union Jack painted on the roof—couldn't get

my driver's license back, rotten luck! five-day waiting period! so she drove; with every gear change her hand ended up on my — oh! sorry, darling, wrong lever! — well, fuck my mother, if I were at the wheel she wouldn't be keeping her eye on the road; she would already be busy getting my sacral chakra opened up — okay, let's calm down — did you see them, those old phonies? blubbering like little brats? what were they hoping for? that you'd get seven years? you'd go down? thanks to their clown of a lawyer from some law firm in some bumfuck place in Charentes? — as it was, thank God we were not riding in this crate of yours, which may go like a bomb, but if that crazy broad had landed on the hood at 150 kph she'd have gone straight through the windshield and killed us dead, the idiot! — I'm finished with that; from now on I'm driving nothing but 4x4's — that demented chick, Sophia Levi, right? well, all she did was bend the fender and dent the grille, period! it was simple, the airbags didn't even come out, I might as well have run over a branch, at most — even pedestrians can be dangerous — apart from the feet and arms, which were still intact — no, actually not, only the left hand stuck between the radiator and the power-steering reservoir; the rest was no longer identifiable — the head burst open like an overripe watermelon on the asphalt, torso and pelvis scattered, so to speak, to the four winds, a few bloodstains and what seemed to me like a scrap of offal on the windshield, otherwise nothing — distracted as I was, I could easily have driven on, under the impression that I had whacked a hare that had strayed onto the autoroute — the Volkswagen salesman had warned me that with this model you are traveling in a luxury bunker on four powered wheels! — but the sound of impact is very specific — hitting a rock or a branch produces a sudden snapping sound, clear and distinct, but with bodies, dog, cat, human, the sound is dull, deep, vibrant, as with rubber, a malleable, indistinct, muffled noise — and so, yes, I thought of the hares that abound in the evening on deserted Irish lanes, with their fluorescent, mauve eyes, rushing onto the roadway dazzled, hypnotized by the headlights — in ten minutes, at high speed, you might nail six or seven—that same rubbery, ill-contoured sound—the elasticity of flesh, its density, probably—and thinking of the eyes of rodents put me in mind of Mademoiselle Sophia's look, in the daytime, evening sunshine, bronze autumn light—5:03 p.m.!—not mauve, phosphorescent eyes, for sure, but big green eyes staring at me, looking for me, but the windshield was tinted, almost black; she could not have seen my face before she died—what energy there was in her eyes!—death was here, and her look said so—Serge Chouraqui, my partner in our import-export business, who always knows the most amazing stuff, told me that in the nineteenth century scientists claimed that the face of the murderer was imprinted, like a photographic image, on the victim's dilated pupil—you just had to examine the iris, explore the crystalline lens, and you would find the criminal—so hold it! prudence is called for!—top-notch advice: (1) rape the woman from behind; (2) cut her throat afterward without ever letting her look around. That it, Serge? or maybe a pillow over the bitch's face before turning the light on?—but anyway, when it came to Sophia Levi, if ever they found her eyes, the enduring retinal image would be of the gleaming metal-gray front of my turbo diesel Volkswagen Tuareg V12—as the toreros say, it is more noble to be gored by a celebrated bull—given the ABS and the lack of any traces of braking on the ground, it proved very hard to estimate the vehicle's speed at the moment of impact—I was doing 220 kph, give or take—must have struck her at 140, I suppose, or at least somewhere between 120 and 150—plus the nature of the damage to a human body, per the court's expert, does not help assess a vehicle's speed—impossible therefore to demonstrate that I was driving too fast—there is a fairly sharp bend at that point, coming just before a long, steep descent, hard to anticipate things, even in a jacked-up 4x4! in short, a tragic concatenation of circumstances—no shit, Sherlock!—come on! drive! keep driving!—no, Jennifer, stop! we don't have the time, for Christ's sake! the first traffic light is just up ahead—so obstinate!—went into cruise control, undid my fly, pulled out my instrument, rubbing it with an expert touch, sizing it up, her beautiful face expressionless, her eyes behind her dark glasses riveted to the road, her skin velvety soft—cut it out! you little slut! in forty-eight seconds we'll be coming into Rambouillet!—I stuffed my junk back into its package, the lawyers' Vel Satis close behind—in five minutes we were at La Chardonnay—*petits toasts*, caviar, champagne galore! Serge, a few business friends, in-laws already there—and after all, the scene I really love, and Jennifer knows it, is me at the wheel, doing 200 kph down the autoroute, she working full-mouthed at my crotch, me putting the car on cruise, opening my chakras to the maximum, picturing monster tits, wet tongues, voluptuous rumps offered up, swollen, moist pussies, Jennifer's and those of others, ah! almost part of the landscape! the windshield a 70-mm screen—come on, faster! all 360 horses! the entire cavalry! ecstasy of speed! intoxication of power! and the combined smells of leather, sperm, and Jean-Paul Gauthier!

16

Rendezvous

I love her, madly, desperately, bask in her light—she enshrouds
me in the aura of her electromagnetic field, her touch suffuses me
with a sweet and tender warmth like that of her belly and inner
thighs—my breathing is affected by it to the point of suffocation
when we are in each other's arms—but the other night as guests
at the house of some friends we found ourselves in a long hallway
embracing, taking advantage of a few moments alone—there was
this damned mirror, and I made the fatal error of raising my head
instead of leaving it safely nestled at her throat in the balm of her
hair—and then suddenly I perceived us as, yes, a couple in fusion,
reflected in the glass—nothing but an empty image—I was shattered,
assailed by a devastating stupor, no longer in her arms, distanced
from myself, from her, from us, in the most brutal way—that image
has become an obstacle for me, a boundary line, and I can no longer
hold her close to me, as though the reflection's glacial magic had
somehow established an unbridgeable gap between us—and so I,
who used always to be on time, if not early, for our appointments,

began coming late, or more accurately on time but given to hiding and, yes, watching her waiting for me before appearing by her side—formerly she was wont to spot me even before approaching with her light step, as though with winged sandals on her adorable feet—the first time she waited for me, alone for five minutes on the Avenue des Gobelins behind a bus shelter's glass partition, I had the chance to observe a sort of astonishment, not to say a wave of anxiety creep across the chiseled features and well-defined bone structure of her face—at my second late arrival I got the feeling, and it upset me, that she was irritated and that her innocence, so well disposed to love, was compromised by the shadow of a doubt—but driven by who knows what devilish mechanism, little by little I increased the length of her wait, progressing from five to fifteen minutes during May—I watched dark shadows accumulating on the sweet contours of her countenance, her smile fading, her élan deflating—her walk altered, she became slow-footed, hesitant, in silhouette hunched slightly, her skin's vitality gone, and her body, once so free, so attuned to what the next moment might bring, so brimful of euphoric energy, was transformed into the afflicting scene of happiness in its death throes, while I, lurking behind a tree, a car, or sometimes ensconced in a dark corner of a café, resisted joining her and felt ravaged by a malaise that was reducing my being to rubble—sometimes, when after too long a wait she left for home, or went to the devil for all I knew, after contemplating her retreating back for a moment I trotted in pursuit and caught up with her out of breath and feeling each time as though I were climbing a higher and higher mountain—and then, in the middle of June, I watched her for nearly twenty-five minutes pacing up and down the sidewalk outside a pharmacy opposite the Salpêtrière Hospital, consulting her watch and trying to call me several times on her cell phone—I had become aware that she was especially agitated, indeed in a cold fury, when all of a sudden she stopped pacing and set off at a run, taking big strides, with all the intensity of sheer flight, and disappeared as she turned right into the Boulevard de Port-Royal—my drink was paid for, and I barged out of the café, shouldering my way past two customers and almost overturning a table as I went, and started running myself, inhabited now by a horrible panic—I covered a hundred yards at top speed before plunging down the boulevard and spotting her at last, two minutes ahead of me, her yellow dress flapping in the wind—I caught up with her, grabbed her arm: so terribly sorry my darling, you have to forgive me—she started in fright and scrutinized me with great green eyes—you are out of your mind! what's the matter with you?!—oh, excuse me, excuse me, Mademoiselle, I was mistaken! I took you—she stared at me, I could see the fear in her look, then she shrugged and went on her way—contemplating her back, its fine curve, my loins urged me to catch up with her again—but for God's sake, she can't have just vanished into thin air! vulture-eyed, I scanned the boulevard once more—ah! there she is! that's her! yes, in a red pleated skirt and a black leather jacket—I dashed across the street, scrambled past the hood of a car braking in a screech of tires, and resumed my chase before she was swallowed up by the metro, getting to her finally, seizing her arm—so very sorry, my darling, please, please forgive me, I—leaping aside, she choked back a scream and turned to me breathlessly: are you crazy? you gave me a fright! you must be nuts!—oh! pardon me please! it's . . . I mistook you for someone else—yes, but then, did she ever come?—will she never come again?

17

The Lord's Day

We were stuck in a traffic jam, it was raining, dismal, the red and white lights wept and streamed with water, I was continually wiping the steamed-up car windows, we were all three trapped, to put it mildly, in a tin box—why on earth had she insisted on coming with him?—excuse me, came her voice from the back, I can't hold off anymore, I have to light up!—she rolled the window down, produced a pack of Gitanes from her pocket, and he, sitting up front in the passenger seat, wriggled and complained—fifty-six years I've had to put up with her cigarette smoke! tobacco makes you sterile, didn't you know that?—when you're seventy-nine years old, what does it matter, sweetheart? I've had two kids, not such a bad score—mother and father were both bundled up in parkas with scarves round their necks, she had a woolen bonnet, he his cap, as though it were unthinkable to take a few things off in the car, the notion probably being that the trip was too short—they looked like hitchhikers getting a five-hundred-meter lift and planning to get out, don skis in the snow, and head for the slopes—just think about it, 12 euros a day for cigarettes! ten days equals 120 euros, twenty equals 240!—okay, I get it, and thirty equals 360, I can figure; don't worry about it, it's my dough—what do you mean, your dough? it's our dough! from the house in Brittany we sold—yes, sweetie, we split it fifty-fifty, so it's my dough—yes, but who restored that house, who fixed it up year after year with blood, sweat, and tears? heck, that's hard to say: blood, sweat, and tears!—and I suppose I did nothing at all in that house?—you? lousy cooking and the dishes, period!—you rotten amnesiac! what about the housework, and the painting, inside and out, and stripping the shutters, and the garden, you name it—We were not so much in a car as in a simmering cauldron of old grudges, sour memories, and resentments bubbling to the surface of a foul broth and bursting: silver wedding, golden wedding, diamond wedding—just a man and a woman, la la la—a silence of several seconds, time to sharpen the knives, reload the pistols and automatic rifles, just a technical pause—the father harrying the mother, a persecution complex in the active voice: he had always put all the blame on her as soon as a tap started dripping, a light bulb blew, or a plate got chipped—he rewrote their entire history from the year dot, blaming her as the "objective cause" of every defeat, every massacre, every betrayal, every extermination, at fault for the effect of the passage of time on every object, every habit—for yellowed leaves falling from a sick tree, or aphids devouring a rose bush, or a kitchen-floor tile breaking loose—he would indict her, find her guilty; there might be an hour or an entire morning of vituperation before he finally slammed the door and went out walking, wandering in the local streets—some neighbor would bring him home, leading him by the hand like a lost child, by which time he had forgotten the whole thing, took her in his arms, and talked to her like a young lover, trying to kiss her while she still seethed—so they had sold the house in Brittany, divided the meager haul, and now she lived in a two-room apartment ten minutes from me, and he, so prone to getting lost in town, to meandering into future and past with little notion of the present, led a cloistered existence in a modest retirement home, cost 2,600 euros a month, his third such in as many years, so great was his corrosive effect on his surroundings and the rules that held sway there—she was sometimes tempted to take him back into her flat, but she had grown as frail as a butterfly in the wake of a pulmonary embolism, just after their move—which explains why I was getting them together every Sunday at her place or mine—I would park in the lot on the grounds of the home, a place of dusty trees rimmed by the long public-housing projects of the fine town of Eaubonne—the establishment is called the Montjoie Residence, the name spelled out in fuchsia letters on a turquoise background—I would spot him at the window of his second-floor room, on the lookout for me since seven in the morning, a two-and-a-half-hour wasted vigil every Sunday, the day that God did not create because He was resting—it was useless repeating to the old man that I came at nine or nine-thirty—I would get out of the car, approach the building entrance, we would wave to each other, he'd be shaved, his hair brushed, white shirt, cherry-red tie, blazer—no sooner was I in the lobby than I was assailed by smells of Lysol, Dakin's solution, and rank old skin—I climbed the stairs, passing shriveled, gray, rumpled, hunched figures talking loudly, alone, in pairs or in groups . . . I entered his room, he smiled and threw his arms around me, redolent with lavender water, and though ready above the waist, below he would still be in bedroom slippers and striped pajama pants stinking of old piss, and this despite my more and more emphatic complaints to the staff, who failed to change his clothes or mislaid them . . . once I got him fully dressed we set off back toward Paris, he singing, whistling, and voicing astonishment at everything: late-model cars, buildings, intersections, bridges, supermarkets, every time as though he had just been let out of prison after being locked up for thirty years—then he would become extremely excited by number and letter games: car license plates with three letters? did you see that? LHO? look! and there's an MAG! and a 74, isn't that the code for Savoie? oh, I give up: 63? what department is that? this would wear him out after ten minutes or so, and pointing, he would punctuate the remainder of the trip with barked binary orders: stop, son, a red light! go, it's green!—once we arrived, he would kiss his wife as though he had just been out to get croissants for breakfast, as if they were still living together, then make himself at home, pacing around the two-room flat: the windows needed reputtying, a tap had to have a new washer, they needed a new spaghetti strainer—sometimes he went out to the hardware store down the street, purchased the necessary items, rolled up his sleeves, and went to work—on this particular evening, who knew why, she had wanted to come along on the return trip, stubborn as a mule! quite impossible to dissuade her!—alright then, the weapons are ready! let the games begin!—all the same, that makes 360 euros going up in smoke every single month; do you know what that comes to in a year? figure over fifty-six years, okay? have you added it up? think of it! we could be living in a palace with its own grounds and a swimming pool!—yes, that's right! then you could have all your girlfriends over, all those secretaries, bank tellers, girls from the vegetable stand or the bakery, mothers waiting for their kids outside school, mail carriers, lady cops, and on and on—you could have your filthy way with them in the bushes, or openly by the pool for that matter—can't you just see them all there together? you filthy old lecher!—I myself suspect my father suffered from priapism—he used to jump on any woman who came within range of his prick; he could sense when a female was in heat (as he put it)—he had a handsome face, great charm, a winning smile, and the laughter-inducing patter that went with them—his wife, whom he possessed like a mad dog almost daily, was not enough for him—had he been a herder high in some summer pasture he would have fucked his donkey, his dog, and his goats—it was raining more heavily now, we had advanced only three hundred meters in ten minutes, the damned windows were still misting up, the stink of dark tobacco filled the car—it was not just one cigarette; she had fired up a third, her window wide open—we are cold for shit's sake! he groaned—and turning to me: she is a real bitch, your mother, she really pisses me off! you know why she kicked me out? do you want to know? because I can't get it up any more! it's true, wouldn't you call that cruelty?—well, of course, at eighty-five fatigue may set in, I replied sympathetically—no, you don't get it at all, son! it is since my second prostate operation, in May 2004, that was it, the merry month of May, ha ha ha!—couldn't get it up; the first op didn't do that—they might as well have castrated me those stinking surgeons—eunuchs, jealous wimps is what they were!—there it was though, I couldn't get it up, and that cow, your mother, couldn't hack it—she's a hot one you know, you can take it from me!—so she kicked me out in short order, that's all!—but it was no fault of mine, certainly not!—I checked my mother's reflection in the rearview mirror—she was white, her face a plaster mask as she sucked on her cigarette and gathered her weaponry, her Uzi, her rocket launcher, her fragmentation bombs—aargh! I've had it, this is revolting, I can't take it anymore! croaked my father with one hand on the door handle, which he suddenly operated, deftly unbuckling his seat belt with the other hand as he did so, and there he was, out of the car under the rain, in the middle of the highway zigzagging between the lines of stopped cars—he has gone crazy, darling! he'll get himself killed! get after him! catch him!—I switched the emergency flashers on, shot from the vehicle like a jack-in-a-box—a motor scooter braked in extremis, its front wheel striking my leg and its handlebars jamming themselves into the car door, the rider losing his balance, falling, getting to his feet, insulting me roundly, calling me a murderer: one more second and it would have been a really serious accident—mumbling profuse apologies I rushed off, threading my way between the fenders, I'd shed some outer clothing inside the car, I was in shirtsleeves, already drenched by the time I reached the hard shoulder—he was a hundred meters ahead, trotting along and waving his arms wildly—I sprinted after him, my sopping clothes sticking to me and slowing me down, the exhaust fumes almost choking me, an invisible, viscous layer coating everything with an oily film and burning my throat and eyes . . . he was screaming now, denouncing this dog's life, denouncing a God that didn't hear him, always too busy with other things—I caught his arm, stop! but he went on, struggling, leaving his parka in my hands and heading off again in just his pullover—I grabbed his shoulders, holding him fast, stop!—he turned to face me, looked at me as if he had never seen me before, then collapsed into my arms shuddering, desperate—why have you abandoned me, son? why?—I am here, I am here, come on, get your coat on! horns wailed behind us; our car stood motionless like a stone in the middle of a stream—I held his big calloused hand in mine; he followed me, docile—the traffic was moving forward again, at a crawl; it was hard to get through—the car was an island, a raft amid a steaming river of mechanical lava—when we reached it I loaded my father into his seat, went round the other side, slid behind the wheel shivering with cold, put the heater on, and started off again in a leaden silence—my mother had tossed her butt away, rolled up her window, and closed her eyes—he was stricken, his eyes fixed on the road ahead as if it were a desert we had to cross—forty minutes later we entered the grounds of the Montjoie Residence, we had arrived—what are we doing here, he murmured, why am I here?—don't you remember?—no, why am I here?—that's why you're here, Papa, because you don't remember.

CPSIA information can be obtained at www.ICGtesting.com
Printed in the USA
BVOW03s0903080615

403477BV00001B/5/P